That was the problem with Sam.

He was exactly the kind of man she didn't like. He was cocky, rough and crude. However, there was something about the way he looked in a tight T-shirt that made a mockery of all that very certain hatred.

"Are you going to take off your coat and stay a while?" That question, asked in a faintly mocking tone, sent a dart of tension straight between her thighs.

She could *not* take off her coat. Because she was wearing nothing more than a scrap of red lace underneath it. And now, it was all she could think of. About how little stood between Sam and her naked body.

About what might happen if she just went ahead and dropped the coat and revealed all of that to him.

"It's cold," she snapped.

The maddening man raised his eyebrows, shooting her a look that clearly said *suit yourself*, then set about looking for the fuse box.

She let out an exasperated sigh and followed his path, stopping when she saw him examining the little black switches inside the box.

"It's not a fuse. That means there's something else going on." He slammed the door shut. Then he turned back to look at her. "You should come to my cabin."

* * *

Hold Me, Cowboy is part of the
Copper Ridge series from *New York Times*
bestselling author Maisey Yates

Dear Reader,

I'm delighted to welcome you back to Copper Ridge, Oregon. This series is all about community, family, love and hot cowboys. And in *Hold Me, Cowboy*, it's Christmas in Copper Ridge, which means sparkling lights, chilly days and even colder nights. Except the hero and heroine in this book have found a way to make the nights a whole lot warmer!

I always enjoy writing a book where opposites attract. Because the explosion when irritation turns to passion is always so incredibly intense.

That's just one of the many reasons that I had to pair my rough blacksmith hero, Sam McCormack, with prickly socialite Madison West. The two of them push all the wrong buttons in each other. But they push all the right ones, too. And when a snowstorm sees them both stranded up in the mountains, all that simmering anger turns into something else entirely. They figure having twelve passionate nights before Christmas to burn off all that attraction should be just about perfect. But in the end, it may not be so easy to walk away.

If you enjoy Maddy and Sam and your time in Copper Ridge, I hope you'll check out more stories in the series. Also from Harlequin Desire is *Take Me, Cowboy*, which features Sam's brother Chase. And you can read about the rest of the West family in *One Night Charmer*, *Tough Luck Hero* and *Last Chance Rebel*, out now from HQN Books.

Happy reading!

Maisey

MAISEY YATES

———

HOLD ME, COWBOY

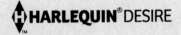
HARLEQUIN®DESIRE

Recycling programs
for this product may
not exist in your area.

ISBN-13: 978-0-373-73492-4

Hold Me, Cowboy

Printed in U.S.A.

Maisey Yates is a *USA TODAY* bestselling author of more than thirty romance novels. She has a coffee habit she has no interest in kicking, and a slight Pinterest addiction. She lives with her husband and children in the Pacific Northwest. When Maisey isn't writing she can be found singing in the grocery store, shopping for shoes online and probably not doing dishes. Check out her website, www.maiseyyates.com.

Books by Maisey Yates

Harlequin Desire

Copper Ridge

Take Me, Cowboy
Hold Me, Cowboy

HQN Books

Copper Ridge

Shoulda Been a Cowboy
Part Time Cowboy
Brokedown Cowboy
Bad News Cowboy
A Copper Ridge Christmas
Take Me, Cowboy
One Night Charmer

Harlequin Presents

Bound to the Warrior King
His Diamond of Convenience
To Defy a Sheikh

Visit her Author Profile page on Harlequin.com, or maiseyyates.com, for more titles!

To KatieSauce, the sister I was always waiting for.
What a joy it is to have you in my life.

One

"Creative photography," Madison West muttered as she entered the security code on the box that contained the key to the cabin she would be staying in for the weekend.

She looked across the snowy landscape to see another home situated *far* too close to the place she would be inhabiting for the next couple of days. The photographs on the vacation-rental website hadn't mentioned that she would be sharing the property with anyone else.

And obviously, the example pictures had been taken from inventive angles.

It didn't matter. Nothing was going to change her plans. She just hoped the neighbors had earplugs. Because she was having sex this weekend. Nonstop sex.

Ten years celibate, and it was ending tonight. She had finally found *the one*. Not the one she was going to marry, obviously. *Please*. Love was for other people. People who hadn't been tricked, manipulated and humiliated when they were seventeen.

No, she had no interest in love and marriage. But she had abundant interest in orgasms. So much interest. And she had found the perfect man to deliver them.

All day, all night, for the next forty-eight hours.

She was armed with a suitcase full of lingerie and four bottles of wine. Neighbors be damned. She'd been hoping for a little more seclusion, but this was fine. It would be fine.

She unlocked the door and stepped inside, breathing a sigh of relief when she saw that the interior, at least, met with her expectations. But it was a little bit smaller than it had looked online, and she could only hope that wasn't some sort of dark portent for the rest of her evening.

She shook her head; she was not going to introduce that concern into the mix, thank you very much. There was enough to worry about when you were thinking about breaking ten years of celibacy without adding such concerns.

Christopher was going to arrive soon, so she figured she'd better get upstairs and start setting a scene. She made her way to the bedroom, then opened her suitcase and took out the preselected bit of lace she had chosen for their first time. It was red, which looked very good on her, if a bit obvious. But she was aiming for obvious.

Christopher wasn't her boyfriend. And he wasn't going to be. He was a very nice equine-vitamin-supplement salesman she'd met a few weeks ago when he'd come by the West estate. She had bought some products for her horses, and they'd struck up a conversation, which had transitioned into a flirtation.

Typically, when things began to transition into flirtation, Maddy put a stop to them. But she hadn't with him. Maybe because he was special. Maybe because ten years was just way too long. Either way, she had kept on flirting with him.

They'd gone out for drinks, and she'd allowed him to kiss her. Which had been a lot more than she'd allowed any other guy in recent years. It had reminded her how much she'd enjoyed that sort of thing once upon a time. And once she'd been reminded…well.

He'd asked for another date. She'd stopped him. Because wouldn't a no-strings physical encounter be way better?

He'd of course agreed. Because he was a man.

But she hadn't wanted to get involved with anyone in town. She didn't need anyone seeing her at a hotel or his house or with his car parked at her little home on her parents' property.

Thus, the cabin-weekend idea had been born.

She shimmied out of her clothes and wiggled into the skintight lace dress that barely covered her backside. Then she set to work fluffing her blond hair and applying some lipstick that matched the lingerie.

She was not answering the door in this outfit, however.

She put her long coat back on over the lingerie, then gave her reflection a critical look. It had been a long time since she had dressed to attract a man. Usually, she was more interested in keeping them at a distance.

"Not tonight," she said. "*Not* tonight."

She padded downstairs, peering out the window and seeing nothing beyond the truck parked at the small house across the way and a vast stretch of snow, falling harder and faster.

Typically, it didn't snow in Copper Ridge, Oregon. You had to drive up to the mountains—as she'd done today—to get any of the white stuff. So, for her, this was a treat, albeit a chilly one. But that was perfect, since she planned to get her blood all heated and stuff.

She hummed, keeping an eye on the scene outside, waiting for Christopher to pull in. She wondered if she should have brought a condom downstairs with her. Decided that she should have.

She went back upstairs, taking them two at a time, grateful that she was by herself, since there was nothing sexy about her ascent. Then she rifled through her bag, found some protection and curled her fingers around it before heading back down the stairs as quickly as possible.

As soon as she entered the living area, the lights flickered, then died. Suddenly, everything in the house seemed unnaturally quiet, and even though it was probably her imagination, she felt the temperature drop several degrees.

"Are you kidding me?" she asked, into the darkness.

There was no answer. Nothing but a subtle creak from the house. Maybe it was all that heavy snow on the roof. Maybe it was going to collapse. That would figure.

A punishment for her thinking she could be normal and have sex.

A shiver worked its way down her spine, and she jolted.

Suddenly, she had gone from hopeful and buoyant to feeling a bit flat and tragic. That was definitely not the best sign.

No. She wasn't doing this. She wasn't sinking into self-pity and tragedy. Been there, done that for ten years, thank you.

Madison didn't believe in signs. *So there.* She believed in fuses blowing in bad weather when overtaxed heaters had to work too hard in ancient houses. Yes, *that* she believed in. She also believed that she would have to wait for Christopher to arrive to fix the problem.

She sighed and then made her way over to the kitchen counter and grabbed hold of her purse as she deposited the two condoms on the counter. She pulled her phone out and grimaced when she saw that she had no signal.

Too late, she remembered that she had thought the lack of cell service might be an attraction to a place like this. That it would be nice if both she and Christopher could be cut off from the outside world while they indulged themselves.

That notion seemed really freaking stupid right now. Since she couldn't use the phone in the house thanks to the outage, and that left her cut off from the outside world all alone.

"Oh no," she said, "I'm the first five minutes of a crime show. I'm going to get ax-murdered. And I'm going to die a born-again virgin."

She scowled, looking back out at the resolutely blank landscape. Christopher still wasn't here. But it looked like the house across the way had power.

She pressed her lips together, not happy about the idea of interrupting her neighbor. Or of meeting her neighbor, since the whole point of going out of town was so they could remain anonymous and not see people.

She tightened the belt on her coat and made her way slowly out the front door, bracing herself against the arctic wind.

She muttered darkly about the cold as she made her way across the space between the houses. She paused for a moment in front of the larger cabin, lit up and looking all warm and toasty. Clearly, this was the pre-

mium accommodation. While hers was likely beset
by rodents that had chewed through relevant cords.

She huffed, clutching her coat tightly as she
knocked on the door. She waited, bouncing in place
to try to keep her blood flowing. She just needed to
call Christopher and find out when he would be ar-
riving and, if he was still a ways out, possibly beg
her neighbor for help getting the power going. Or at
least help getting a fire started.

The front door swung open and Madison's heart
stopped. The man standing there was large, so tall
that she only just came up to the middle of his chest.
He was broad, his shoulders well muscled, his waist
trim. He had the kind of body that came not from
working out but from hard physical labor.

Then she looked up. Straight nose, square jaw,
short brown hair and dark eyes that were even harder
than his muscles. And far too familiar.

"What are *you* doing here?"

Sam McCormack gritted his teeth against the sharp
tug of irritation that assaulted him when Madison
West asked the question that had been on his own lips.

"I rented the place," he responded, not inviting
her in. "Though I could ask you the same question."

She continued to do a little bounce in place, her
arms folded tight against her body, her hands clasped
beneath her chin. "And you'd get the same answer,"
she said. "I'm across the driveway."

"Then you're at the wrong door." He made a move to shut said door, and she reached out, stopping him.

"Sam. Do you always have to be this unpleasant?"

It was a question that had been asked of him more than once. And he gave his standard answer. "Yes."

"Sam," she said, sounding exasperated. "The power went out, and I'm freezing to death. Can I come in?"

He let out a long-suffering sigh and stepped to the side. He didn't like Madison West. He never had. Not from the moment he had been hired on as a farrier for the West estate eight years earlier. In all the years since he'd first met Madison, since he'd first started shoeing her horses, he'd never received one polite word from her.

But then, he'd never given one either.

She was sleek, blonde and freezing cold—and he didn't mean because she had just come in from the storm. The woman carried her own little snow cloud right above her head at all times, and he wasn't a fan of ice princesses. Still, something about her had always been like a burr beneath his skin that he couldn't get at.

"Thank you," she said crisply, stepping over the threshold.

"You're rich and pretty," he said, shutting the door tight behind her. "And I'm poor. And kind of an ass. It wouldn't do for me to let you die out there in a snowdrift. I would probably end up getting hung."

Madison sniffed, making a show of brushing

snowflakes from the shoulders of her jacket. "I highly doubt you're poor," she said drily.

She wasn't wrong. A lot had changed since he'd gone to work for the Wests eight years ago. Hell, a lot had changed in the past year.

The strangest thing was that his art had taken off, and along with it the metalwork and blacksmithing business he ran with his brother, Chase.

But now he was busier coming up with actual fine-art pieces than he was doing daily grunt work. One sale on a piece like that could set them up for the entire quarter. Strange, and not where he'd seen his life going, but true.

He still had trouble defining himself as an artist. In his mind, he was just a blacksmith cowboy. Most at home on the family ranch, most proficient at pounding metal into another shape. It just so happened that for some reason people wanted to spend a lot of money on that metal.

"Well," he said, "perception is everything."

She looked up at him, those blue eyes hitting him hard, like a punch in the gut. That was the other obnoxious thing about Madison West. She was pretty. She was more than pretty. She was the kind of pretty that kept a man up all night, hard and aching, with fantasies about her swirling in his head.

She was also the kind of woman who would probably leave icicles on a man's member after a blow job.

No, thank you.

"Sure," she said, waving her hand. "Now, I *perceive* that I need to use your phone."

"There's no cell service up here."

"Landline," she said. "I have no power. And no cell service. The source of all my problems."

"In that case, be my guest," he responded, turning away from her and walking toward the kitchen, where the lone phone was plugged in.

He picked up the receiver and held it out to her. She eyed it for a moment as though it were a live snake, then snatched it out of his hand. "Are you just going to stand there?"

He shrugged, crossing his arms and leaning against the doorframe. "I thought I might."

She scoffed, then dialed the number, doing the same impatient hop she'd been doing outside while she waited for the person on the other end to answer. "Christopher?"

The physical response Sam felt to her uttering another man's name was not something he ever could have anticipated. His stomach tightened, dropped, and a lick of flame that felt a hell of a lot like jealousy sparked inside him.

"What do you mean you can't get up here?" She looked away from him, determinedly so, her eyes fixed on the kitchen floor. "The road is closed. Okay. So that means I can't get back down either?" There was a pause. "Right. Well, hopefully I don't freeze to death." Another pause. "No, you don't need to call anybody. I'm not going to freeze to death. I'm using the neighbor's phone. Just forget it. I don't have cell service. I'll call you if the power comes back on in my cabin."

She hung up then, her expression so sharp it could have cut him clean through.

"I take it you had plans."

She looked at him, her eyes as frosty as the weather outside. "Did you figure that out all by yourself?"

"Only just barely. You know blacksmiths aren't known for their deductive reasoning skills. Mostly we're famous for hitting heavy things with other heavy things."

"Kind of like cavemen and rocks."

He took a step toward her. "Kind of."

She shrank back, a hint of color bleeding into her cheeks. "Well, now that we've established that there's basically no difference between you and a Neanderthal, I better get back to my dark, empty cabin. And hope that you aren't a secret serial killer."

Her sharp tongue left cuts behind, and he had to admit he kind of enjoyed it. There weren't very many people who sparred with him like this. Possibly because he didn't talk to very many people. "Is that a legitimate concern you have?"

"I don't know. The entire situation is just crazy enough that I might be trapped in a horror movie with a tortured artist blacksmith who is also secretly murdery."

"I guarantee you I'm not murdery. If you see me

outside with an ax, it will only be because I'm cutting firewood."

She cocked her head to the side, a glint in her blue eyes that didn't look like ice making his stomach—and everything south of there—tighten. "Well, that's a relief. Anyway. I'm going. Dark cabin, no one waiting for me. It promises to be a seriously good time."

"You don't have any idea why the power is out, or how to fix it?" he asked.

"No," she said, sounding exasperated, and about thirty seconds away from stamping her foot.

Well, damn his conscience, but he wasn't letting her go back to an empty, dark, cold cabin. No matter that she had always treated him like a bit of muck she'd stepped in with her handmade riding boots.

"Let me have a look at your fuse box," he said.

"You sound like you'd rather die," she said.

"I pretty much would, but I'm not going to let *you* die either." He reached for his black jacket and the matching black cowboy hat hanging on a hook. He put both on and nodded.

"Thank you," she muttered, and he could tell the little bit of social nicety directed at him cost her dearly.

They headed toward the front door and he pushed it open, waiting for her to go out first. Since he had arrived earlier today, the temperature had dropped drastically. He had come up to the mountain to do some planning for his next few art projects. It pained him to admit, even to himself, that solitude was somewhat necessary for him to get a clear handle on what he was going to work on next.

"So," he said, making conversation not so much for the sake of it but more to needle her and see if he could earn one of her patented death glares, "Christopher, huh? Your boyfriend?" That hot spike drove its way through his gut again and he did his best to ignore it.

"No," she said tersely. "Just a friend."

"I see. So you decided to meet a man up here for a friendly game of Twister?"

She turned slightly, arching one pale brow. "Yahtzee, actually. I'm very good at it."

"And I'm sure your...*friend* was hoping to get a full house."

She rolled her eyes and looked forward again, taking quick steps over the icy ground, and somehow managing to keep sure footing. Then she opened the door to her cabin. "Welcome." she said, extending her arm. "Please excuse the shuddering cold and oppressive darkness."

"Ladies first," he said.

She shook her head, walking into the house, and he followed behind, closing the door against the elements. It was already cold in the dark little room. "You were just going to come back here and sit in the dark if I hadn't offered to fiddle with the circuit breaker?"

"Maybe I know how to break my own circuits, Sam. Did you ever think of that?"

"Oh, but you said you didn't, Madison."

"I prefer Maddy," she said.

"Sorry, Madison," he said, tipping his hat, just to be a jerk.

"I should have just frozen to death. Then there could have been a legend about my tragic and beautiful demise in the mountains." He didn't say anything. He just looked at her until she sighed and continued talking. "I don't know where the box thingy is. You're going to have to hunt for it."

"I think I can handle that." He walked deeper into the kitchen, then stopped when he saw two purple packets sitting on the kitchen counter. That heat returned with a vengeance when he realized exactly what they were, and what they meant. He looked up, his eyes meeting her extremely guilty gaze. "Yahtzee, huh?"

"That's what the kids call it," she said, pressing her palm over the telling packets.

"Only because they're too immature to call it fucking."

Color washed up her neck, into her cheeks. "Or not crass enough."

In that moment, he had no idea what devil possessed him, and he didn't particularly care. He turned to face her, planting his hands on the countertop, just an inch away from hers. "I don't know about that. I'm betting that you could use a little crassness in your life, Madison West."

"Are you trying to suggest that I need *you*?" she asked, her voice choked.

Lightning streaked through his blood, and in that moment, he was lost. It didn't matter that he thought she was insufferable, a prissy little princess who didn't appreciate any damn thing she had. It didn't matter that he'd come up here to work.

All that mattered was he hadn't touched a woman in a long time, and Madison West was so close all he would have to do was shift his weight slightly and he'd be able to take her into his arms.

He looked down pointedly at her hand, acting as though he could see straight through to the protection beneath. "Well," he said, "you have a couple of the essential ingredients to have yourself a pretty fun evening. All you seem to be missing is the man. But I imagine the guy you invited up here is *nice*. I'm not very nice, Madison," he said, leaning in, "but I could damn sure show you a good time."

Two

The absolute worst thing was the fact that Sam's words sent a shiver down her spine. Sam McCormack. Why did it have to be Sam McCormack? He was the deadly serpent to her Indiana Jones.

She should throw him out. Throw him out and get back to her very disappointing evening where all orgasms would be self-administered. So, basically a regular Friday night.

She wanted to throw herself on the ground and wail. It was not supposed to be a regular Friday night. She was supposed to be breaking her sex fast. Maybe this was why people had flings in the spring. Inclement weather made winter flings difficult. Also, mostly you just wanted to keep your socks on the whole time. And that wasn't sexy.

Maybe her libido should hibernate for a while. Pop up again when the pear trees were blooming or something.

She looked over at Sam, and her libido made a dash to the foreground. That was the problem with Sam. He irritated her. He was exactly the kind of man she didn't like. He was cocky. He was rough and crude.

Whenever she'd given him very helpful pointers about handling the horses when he came to do far-rier work at the estate, he was always telling her to go away and in general showing no deference.

And okay, if he'd come and told her how to do her job, she would have told him where he could stick his hoof nippers. But still. Her animals. So she was entitled to her opinions.

Last time she'd walked into the barn when he was doing shoes, he hadn't even looked up from his work. He'd just pointed back toward the door and shouted, *out!*

Yeah, he was a jerk.

However, there was something about the way he looked in a tight T-shirt, his muscles bulging as he did all that hard labor, that made a mockery of that very certain hatred she felt burning in her breast.

"Are you going to take off your coat and stay awhile?" The question, asked in a faintly mocking tone, sent a dart of tension straight down between her thighs.

She could *not* take off her coat. Because she was

wearing nothing more than a little scrap of red lace underneath it. And now that was all she could think of. About how little stood between Sam and her naked body.

About what might happen if she just went ahead and dropped the coat now and revealed all of that to him.

"It's cold," she snapped. "Maybe if you went to work getting the electricity back on rather than standing there making terrible double entendres, I would be able to take off my coat."

He lifted a brow. "And then do you think you'll take me up on my offer to show you a good time?"

"If you can get my electricity back on, I will consider a good time shown to me. Honestly, that's all I want. The ability to microwave popcorn and not turn into a Maddycicle."

The maddening man raised his eyebrows, shooting her a look that clearly said *Suit yourself*, then set about looking for the fuse box.

She stood by alone for a while, her arms wrapped around her midsection. Then she started to feel like an idiot just kind of hanging out there while he searched for the source of all power. She let out an exasperated sigh and followed his path, stopping when she saw him leaning up against a wall, a little metal door fixed between the logs open as he examined the small black switches inside.

"It's not a fuse. That means there's something else going on." He slammed the door shut. Then he turned back to look at her. "You should come over to my cabin."

"No!" The denial was a little bit too enthusiastic. A little bit too telling. "I mean, I can start a fire here—it's going to be fine. I'm not going to freeze."

"You're going to curl up by the fire with a blanket? Like a sad little pet?"

She made a scoffing sound. "No, I'm going to curl up by the fire like the Little Match Girl."

"That makes it even worse. The Little Match Girl froze to death."

"What?"

"How did you not know that?"

"I saw it when I was a kid. It was a *cartoon*. She really died?" Maddy blinked. "What kind of story is that to present to children?"

"An early lesson, maybe? Life is bleak, and then you freeze to death alone?"

"Charming," she said.

"Life rarely is." He kept looking at her. His dark gaze was worrisome.

"I'm fine," she said, because somebody had to say something.

"You are not. Get your suitcase—come over to the cabin. We can flip the lights on, and then if we notice from across the driveway that your power's on again, you can always come back."

It was stupid to refuse him. She knew him, if not personally, at least well enough to know that he wasn't any kind of danger to her.

The alternative was trying to sleep on the couch in the living room while the outside temperatures hovered below freezing, waking up every few hours to keep the fire stoked.

Definitely, going over to his cabin made more sense. But the idea filled her with a strange tension that she couldn't quite shake. Well, she knew exactly what kind of tension it was. *Sexual tension.*

She and Sam had so much of it that hung between them like a fog whenever they interacted. Although, maybe she read it wrong. Maybe on his end it was just irritation and it wasn't at all tinged with sensual shame.

"Why do you have to be so damned reasonable?" she asked, turning away from him and stalking toward the stairs.

"Where are you going?"

She stopped, turning to face him. "To change. Also, to get my suitcase. I have snacks in there."

"Are snacks a euphemism for something interesting?" he asked, arching a dark brow.

She sputtered, genuinely speechless. Which was unusual to downright unheard of. "No," she said, her tone sounding petulant. "I have *actual snacks.*"

"Come over to my place. Bring the snacks."

"I will," she said, turning on her heel, heading toward the stairs.

"Maybe bring the Yahtzee too."

Those words hit her hard, with all the impact of a stomach punch. She could feel her face turning crimson, and she refused to look back at him. Refused to react to that bait at all. He didn't want *that*. He did not want to play euphemistic board games with her. And she didn't want to play them with him.

If she felt a little bit...on edge, it was just because she had been anticipating sex and she had experienced profound sex disappointment. That was all.

She continued up the stairs, making her way to the bedroom, then changed back into a pair of jeans and a sweatshirt as quickly as possible before stuffing the little red lace thing back in the bag and zipping everything up.

She lugged it back downstairs, her heart slamming against her breastbone when Sam was in her line of sight again. Tall, broad shouldered and far too sexy for his own good, he promised to be the antidote to sexual disappointment.

But an emotionless hookup with a guy she liked well enough but wouldn't get emotionally involved with was one thing. Replacing him at the last moment with a guy she didn't even like? No, that was out of the question.

Absolutely and completely out of the question.

"Okay," she said, "let's go."

By the time she got settled in the extra room in the cabin, she was feeling antsy. She could hide, but she was hungry. And Maddy didn't believe in being hungry when food was at hand. Yes, she had some various sugar-based items in her bag, but she needed protein.

In the past, she had braved any number of her father's awkward soirees to gain access to bacon-wrapped appetizers.

She could brave Sam McCormack well enough to root around for sustenance. She would allow no man to stand between herself and her dinner.

Cautiously, she made her way downstairs, hoping that maybe Sam had put himself away for the night. The thought made her smile. That he didn't go to bed like a normal person but closed himself inside…not a coffin. But maybe a scratchy, rock-hewn box that would provide no warmth or comfort. It seemed like something he would be into.

In fairness, she didn't really know Sam McCormack that well, but everything she did know about him led her to believe that he was a supremely unpleasant person. Well, except for the whole him-not-letting-her-die-of-frostbite-in-her-powerless-cabin thing. She supposed she had to go ahead and put that in the Maybe He's Not Such a Jackass column.

Her foot hit the ground after the last stair silently, and she cautiously padded into the kitchen.

"Looking for something?"

She startled, turning around and seeing Sam standing there, leaning in the doorway, his muscular arms crossed over his broad chest. She did her best to look cool. Composed. Not interested in his muscles. "Well—" she tucked her hair behind her ear "—I was hoping to find some food."

"You brought snacks," he said.

"Candy," she countered.

"So, that made it okay for you to come downstairs and steal my steak?"

Her stomach growled. "You have steak?"

"It's *my* steak."

She hadn't really thought of that. "Well, my...you know, *the guy*. He was supposed to bring food. And I'm sorry. I didn't exactly think about the fact that whatever food is in this fridge is food that you personally provided. I was protein blind." She did her best to look plaintive. Unsurprisingly, Sam did not seem moved by her plaintiveness.

"I mean, it seems cruel to eat steak in front of you, Madison. Especially if I'm not willing to share." He rubbed his chin, the sounds of his whiskers abrading his palm sending a little shiver down her back. God knew why.

"You *would* do that. You would... You would tease me with your steak." Suddenly, it was all starting to sound a little bit sexual. Which she had a feeling was due in part to the fact that everything felt sexual to her right about now.

Which was because of the other man she had been about to sleep with. Not Sam. Not really.

A slow smile crossed his face. "I would never tease you with my steak, Madison. If you want a taste, all you have to do is ask. Nicely."

She felt her face getting hotter. "May I please have your steak?"

"Are you going to cook it for me?"

"Did you want it to be edible?"

"That would be the goal, yes," he responded.

She lifted her hands up, palms out. "These hands don't cook."

His expression shifted. A glint of wickedness cutting through all that hardness. She'd known Sam was mean. She'd known he was rough. She had not realized he was wicked. "What do those hands do, I wonder?"

He let that innuendo linger between them and she practically hissed in response. "Do you have salad? I will fix salad. *You* cook steak. Then we can eat."

"Works for me, but I assume you're going to be sharing your candy with me?"

Seriously, everything sounded filthy. She had to get a handle on herself. "Maybe," she said, "but it depends on if your behavior merits candy." That didn't make it better.

"I see. And what, pray tell, does Madison West consider candy-deserving behavior?"

She shrugged, making her way to the fridge and opening it, bending down and opening the crisper drawer. "I don't know. Not being completely unbearable?"

"Your standards are low."

"Luckily for you."

She looked up at him and saw that that had actually elicited what looked to be a genuine grin. The man was a mystery. And she shouldn't care about that. She should not want to unlock, unravel or otherwise solve him.

The great thing about Christopher was that he was simple. He wasn't connected to her life in any way. They could come up and have an affair and it would never bleed over to her existence in Copper Ridge. It was the antithesis of everything she had experienced with David. David, who had blown up her entire life, shattered her career ambitions and damaged her good standing in the community.

This thing with Christopher was supposed to be sex. Sex that made nary a ripple in the rest of her life.

Sam would not be rippleless.

The McCormack family was too much a part of the fabric of Copper Ridge. More so in the past year. Sam and his brother, Chase, had done an amazing job of revitalizing their family ranch, and somewhere in all of that Sam had become an in-demand artist. Though he would be the last person to say it. He still showed up right on schedule to do the farrier work at her family ranch. As though he weren't raking in way more money with his ironwork.

Sam was… Well, he was kind of everywhere. His works of art appearing in restaurants and galleries around town. His person appearing on the family ranch to work on the horses. He was the exact wrong kind of man for her to be fantasizing about.

She should be more gun-shy than this. Actually,

she had spent the past decade being more gun-shy than this. It was just that apparently now that she had allowed herself to remember she had sexual feelings, it was difficult for her to turn them off. Especially when she was trapped in a snowstorm with a man for whom the term *rock-hard body* would be a mere description and not hyperbole.

She produced the salad, then set about to preparing it. Thankfully, it was washed and torn already. So her responsibility literally consisted of dumping it from bag to bowl. That was the kind of cooking she could get behind. Meanwhile, Sam busied himself with preparing two steaks on the stovetop. At some point, he took the pan from the stovetop and transferred it to the oven.

"I didn't know you had actual cooking technique," she said, not even pretending to herself that she wasn't watching the play of his muscles in his forearms as he worked.

Even at the West Ranch, where she always ended up sniping at him if they ever interacted, she tended to linger around him while he did his work with the horses because his arms put on quite a show. She was hardly going to turn away from him now that they were in an enclosed space, with said arms very, very close. And no one else around to witness her ogling.

She just didn't possess that kind of willpower.

"Well, Madison, I have a lot of eating technique. The two are compatible."

"Right," she said, "as you don't have a wife. Or a

girlfriend…" She could have punched her own face for that. It sounded so leading and obvious. As if she cared if he had a woman in his life.

She didn't. Well, she kind of did. Because honestly, she didn't even like to ogle men who could be involved with another woman. Once bitten, twice shy. By which she meant once caught in a torrid extramarital affair with a man in good standing in the equestrian community, ten years emotionally scarred.

"No," he said, tilting his head, the cocky look in his eye doing strange things to her stomach, "I don't."

"I don't have a boyfriend. Not an actual boyfriend." Oh, good Lord. She was the desperate worst and she hated herself.

"So you keep saying," he returned. "You really want to make sure I know Christopher isn't your boyfriend." She couldn't ignore the implication in his tone.

"Because he isn't. Because we're not… Because we've never. This was going to be our first time." Being forthright and making people uncomfortable with said forthrightness had been a very handy shield for the past decade, but tonight it was really obnoxious.

"Oh really?" He suddenly looked extremely interested.

"Yes," she responded, keeping her tone crisp, refusing to show him just how off-kilter she felt. "I'm just making dinner conversation."

"This is the kind of dinner conversation you normally make?"

She arched her brow. "Actually, yes. Shocking people is kind of my modus operandi."

"I don't find you that shocking, Madison. I do find it a little bit amusing that you got cock-blocked by a snowbank."

She nearly choked. "Wine. Do you have wine?" She turned and started rummaging through the nearest cabinet. "Of course you do. You probably have a baguette too. That seems like something an artist would do. Set up here and drink wine and eat a baguette."

He laughed, a kind of short, dismissive sound. "Hate to disappoint you. But my artistic genius is fueled by Jack." He reached up, opening the cabinet nearest to his head, and pulled down a bottle of whiskey. "But I'm happy to share that too."

"You have diet soda?"

"Regular."

"My, this *is* a hedonistic experience. I'll have regular, then."

"Well, when a woman was expecting sex and doesn't get it, I suppose regular cola is poor consolation, but it is better than diet."

"Truer words were never spoken." She watched him while he set about to making a couple of mixed drinks for them. He handed one to her, and she lifted it in salute before taking a small sip. By then he was taking the steak out of the oven and setting it back on the stovetop.

"Perfect," he remarked when he cut one of the pieces of meat in half and gauged the color of the interior.

She frowned. "How did I never notice that you aren't horrible?"

He looked at her, his expression one of mock surprise. "Not horrible? You be careful throwing around compliments like that, missy. A man could get the wrong idea."

She rolled her eyes. "Right. I just mean, you're funny."

"How much of that whiskey have you had?"

"One sip. So it isn't even that." She eyeballed the food that he was now putting onto plates. "It might be the steak. I'm not going to lie to you."

"I'm comfortable with that."

He carried their plates to the table, and she took the lone bottle of ranch dressing out of the fridge and set it and her drink next to her plate. And then, somehow, she ended up sitting at a very nicely appointed dinner table with Sam McCormack, who was not the man she was supposed to be with tonight.

Maybe it was because of the liquored-up soda. Maybe it was neglected hormones losing their everloving minds in the presence of such a fine male specimen. Maybe it was just as simple as want. Maybe there was no justification for it at all. Except that Sam was actually beautiful. And she had always thought so, no matter how much he got under her skin.

That was the honest truth. It was why she found him so off-putting, why she had always found him so off-putting from the moment he had first walked onto the West Ranch property. Because he was the kind of man a woman could make a mistake with. And she had thought she was done making mistakes.

Now she was starting to wonder if a woman was entitled to one every decade.

Her safe mistake, the one who would lift out of her life, hadn't eventuated. And here in front of her was one that had the potential to be huge. But very, very good.

She wasn't so young anymore. She wasn't naive at all. When it came right down to it, she was hot for Sam. She had been for a long time.

She'd had so much caution for so long. So much hiding. So much *not doing*. Well, she was tired of that.

"I was very disappointed about Christopher not making it up here," she said, just as Sam was putting the last bite of steak into his mouth.

"Sure," he said.

"Very disappointed."

"Nobody likes blue balls, Maddy, even if they don't have testicles."

She forced a laugh through her constricted throat. "That's hilarious," she said.

He looked up at her slowly. "No," he said, "it wasn't."

She let out a long, slow breath. "Okay," she said, "it wasn't that funny. But here's the thing. The reason I was so looking forward to tonight is that I hadn't had sex with Christopher before. In fact, I haven't had sex with anyone in ten years. So. Maybe you could help me with that?"

Three

Sam was pretty sure he must be hallucinating. Because there was no way Madison West had just propositioned him. Especially not on the heels of admitting that it had been ten years since she'd had sex.

Hell, he was starting to think that *he* was the celibacy champion. But clearly, Maddy had him beat. Or she didn't, because there was no way in hell that she had actually said any of that.

"Are you drunk, Madison?" It was the first thing that came to mind, and it seemed like an important thing to figure out.

"After one Jack Daniel's and Coke? Absolutely not. I am a West, dammit. We can hold our liquor. I am…reckless, opportunistic and horny. A lot horny. I just… I need this. Sam, do you know what it's like to go *ten years* without doing something? It becomes a whole thing. Like, a whole big thing that starts to define you, even if it shouldn't. And you don't want anyone to know. Oh, my gosh, can you even imagine if my friends knew that it has been ten years since I have seen an actual…?" She took a deep breath, then forged on. "I'm rambling and I just *really* need this."

Sam felt like he had been hit over the head with a metric ton of iron. He had no idea how he was supposed to respond to this—the strangest of all propositions—from a woman who had professed to hate him only a few moments ago.

He had always thought Madison was a snob. A pain in his ass, even if she was a pretty pain in the ass. She was always looming around, looking down her nose at him while he did his work. As though only the aristocracy of Copper Ridge could possibly know how to do the lowly labor he was seeing to. Even if they hadn't the ability to do it themselves.

The kinds of people who professed to have strengths in "management." People who didn't know how to get their hands dirty.

He hated people like that. And he had never been a fan of Madison West.

He, Sam McCormack, should not be interested in taking her up on her offer. No, not in any way. However, Sam McCormack's dick was way more interested in it than he would've liked to admit.

Immediately, he was rock hard thinking about what it would be like to have her delicate, soft hands skimming over him. He had rough hands. Workman's hands. The kind of hands that a woman like Madison West had probably never felt against her rarefied flesh.

Hell, the fact that it had been ten years since she'd gotten any made that even more likely. And damn if that didn't turn him on. It was kind of twisted, a little bit sick, but then, it was nothing short of what he expected from himself.

He was a lot of things. Good wasn't one of them.

Ready to explode after years of repressing his desires, after years of pushing said desire all down and pretending it wasn't there? He was that.

"I'm not actually sure you want this," he said, wondering what the hell he was doing. Giving her an out when he wanted to throw her down and make her his.

Maddy stood up, not about to be cowed by him. He should have known that she would take that as a challenge. Maybe he had known that. Maybe it was why he'd said it.

That sounded like him. That sounded a lot more like him than trying to do the honorable thing.

"You don't know what I want, Sam," she said, crossing the space between them, swaying her hips just a little bit more than she usually did.

He would be a damn liar if he said that he had never thought about what it might be like to grab hold of those hips and pull Maddy West up against him. To grind his hardness against her soft flesh and make her feel exactly what her snobby-rich-girl mouth did to him.

But just because he'd fantasized about it before, didn't mean he had ever anticipated doing it. It didn't mean that he should take her up on it now.

Still, the closer she got to him, the less likely it seemed that he was going to say no.

"I think that after ten years of celibacy a man could make the argument that you don't know what you want, Madison West."

Her eyes narrowed, glittering blue diamonds that looked like they could cut a man straight down to the bone. "I've always known what I wanted. I may not have always made the best decisions, but I was completely certain that I wanted them. At the time."

His lips tipped upward. "I'm just going to be another *at the time*, Maddy. Nothing else."

"That was the entire point of this weekend. For me to have something that didn't have consequences. For me to get a little bit of something for myself. Is that so wrong? Do I have to live a passionless existence because I made a mistake once? Am I going to question myself forever? I just need to… I need to rip the Band-Aid off."

"The Band-Aid?"

"The sex Band-Aid."

He nodded, pretending that he understood. "Okay."

"I want this," she said, her tone confident.

"Are you…suggesting…that I give you…sexual healing?"

She made a scoffing sound. "Don't make it sound cheesy. This is very serious. I would never joke about my sexual needs." She let out an exasperated sigh. "I'm doing this wrong. I'm just…"

Suddenly, she launched herself at him, wrapping her arms around his neck and pressing her lips against his. The moment she did it, it was like the strike of a hammer against hot iron. As rigid as he'd been before—in that moment, he bent. And easily.

Staying seated in the chair, he curved himself around Madison, wrapping his arms around her body, sliding his hands over her back, down to the sweet indent of her waist, farther still to the flare of those pretty hips. The hips he had thought about taking hold of so many times before.

There was no hesitation now. None at all. There was only this. Only her. Only the soft, intoxicating taste of her on his tongue. Sugar, Jack Daniel's and something that was entirely Maddy.

Too rich for his blood. Far too expensive for a man like him. It didn't matter what he became. Didn't matter how much money he had in his bank account, he would always be what he was. There was no escaping it. Nobody knew. Not really. Not the various women who had graced his bed over the years, not his brother, Chase.

Nobody knew Sam McCormack.

At least, nobody alive.

Neither, he thought, would Madison West. This wasn't about knowing anybody. This was just about satisfying a need. And he was simple enough to take her up on that.

He wedged his thigh up between her legs, pressing his palm down on her lower back, encouraging her to flex her hips in time with each stroke of his tongue. Encouraging her to satisfy that ache at the apex of her thighs.

Her head fell back, her skin flushed and satisfaction grabbed him by the throat, gripping him hard and strong. It would've surprised him if he hadn't suspected he was the sort of bastard who would get off on something like this.

Watching this beautiful, classy girl coming undone in his arms.

She was right. This weekend could be out of time. It could be a moment for them to indulge in things they would never normally allow themselves to have. The kinds of things that he had closed himself off from years ago.

Softness, warmth, touch.

He had denied himself all those things for years. Why not do this now? No one would know. No one would ever have to know. Maddy would see to that. She would never, no chance in hell, admit that she had gotten down and dirty with a man who was essentially a glorified blacksmith.

No way in hell.

That made them both safe. It made this safe. Well, as safe as fire this hot could be.

She bit his lip and he growled, pushing his hands

up underneath the hem of her shirt, kissing her
deeper as he let his fingertips roam to the line of
her elegant spine, then tracing it upward until he
found her bra, releasing it with ease, then dragging
it and her top up over her head, leaving her naked
from the waist up.

"I…" Her face was a bright shade of red. "I…I
have lingerie. I wasn't going to…"

"I don't give a damn about your lingerie. I just
want this." He lowered his head, sliding his tongue
around the perimeter of one of her tightened nipples.
"I want your skin." He closed his lips over that tight
bud, sucking it in deep.

"I had a seduction plan," she said, her voice trembling. He wasn't entirely sure it was a protest, or even
a complaint.

"You don't plan passion, baby," he said.

At least, he didn't. Because if he were thinking
clearly, he would be putting her top back on and telling her to go back to her ice-cold cabin, where she
would be safe.

"I do," she said, her teeth chattering in spite of
the fact that it was very warm in the kitchen. "I plan
everything."

"Not this. You're a dirty girl now, Madison West,"
he said, sliding his thumb over her damp nipple,
moving it in a slow circle until she arched her back
and cried out. "You were going to sleep with another
man this weekend, and you replaced him so damn

easily. With me. Doesn't even matter to you who you have. As long as you get a little bit. Is that how it is?"

She whimpered, biting her lip, rolling her hips against him.

"Good girl," he said, his gut tightening, his arousal so hard he was sure he was going to burst through the front of his jeans. "I like that. I like you being dirty for me."

He moved his hands then, curving his fingers around her midsection, his thumbs resting just beneath the swell of her breasts. She was so soft, so smooth, so petite and fragile. Everything he should never be allowed to put his hands on. But for some reason, instead of feeling a bolt of shame, he felt aroused. Hotter and harder than he could ever remember being. "You like that? My hands are rough. Maybe a little bit too rough for you."

"No," she said, and this time the protest was clear. "Not too rough for me at all."

He slid his hands down her back, taking a moment to really revel in how soft she was and how much different he must feel to her. She squirmed against him, and he took that as evidence that she really did like it.

That only made him hotter. Harder. More impatient.

"You didn't bring your damn candy and forget the condoms, did you?"

"No," she said, the denial coming quickly. "I brought the condoms."

"You always knew we would end up like this, didn't you?"

She looked away from him, and the way she refused to meet his eyes turned a throwaway game of a question into something deadly serious.

"Madison," he said, his voice hard. She still didn't look at him. He grabbed hold of her chin, redirecting her face so that she was forced to make eye contact with him. "You knew this would happen all along, didn't you?"

She still refused to answer him. Refused to speak.

"I think you did," he continued. "I think that's why you can never say a kind word to me. I think that's why you acted like a scalded cat every time I walked into the room. Because you knew it would end here. Because you wanted this. Because you wanted me."

Her expression turned even more mutinous.

"Madison," he said, a warning lacing through the word. "Don't play games with me. Or I'm not going to give you what you want. So you have to tell me. Tell me that you've always wanted me. You've always wanted my dirty hands on you. That's why you hate me so damn much, isn't it? Because you want me."

"I…"

"Madison," he said, his tone even more firm, "tell me—" he rubbed his hand over her nipple "—or I stop."

"I wanted you," she said, the admission rushed but clear all the same.

"More," he said, barely recognizing his own voice. "Tell me more."

It seemed essential suddenly, to know she'd wanted him. He didn't know why. He didn't care why.

"I've always wanted you. From the moment I first saw you. I knew that it would be like this. I knew that I would climb up into your lap and I would make a fool of myself rubbing all over you like a cat. I knew that from the beginning. So I argued with you instead."

He felt a satisfied smile that curved his lips upward. "Good girl." He lowered his hands, undoing the snap on her jeans and drawing the zipper down slowly. "You just made us both very happy." He moved his fingertips down beneath the waistband of her panties, his breath catching in his throat when he felt hot wetness beneath his touch. It had been way too long since he felt a silky-smooth desirable woman. Had been way too long in his self-imposed prison.

Too long since he'd wanted at all.

But Madison wasn't Elizabeth. And this wasn't the same.

He didn't need to think about her. He wasn't going to. Not for the rest of the night.

He pushed every thought out of his mind and instead exulted in the sound that Madison made when he moved his fingers over that place where she was wet and aching for him. When he delved deeper, pushing one finger inside her, feeling just how close she was to the edge, evidenced by the way her internal muscles clenched around him. He could thrust into her here. Take her hard and fast and she would still come. He knew that she would.

But she'd had ten years of celibacy, and he was pushing on five. They deserved more. They deserved better. At the very least they deserved a damn bed.

With that in mind, he wrapped his arms more tightly around her, moving his hands to cup her behind as he lifted her, wrapping her legs tightly around him as he carried them across the kitchen and toward the stairs.

Maddy let out an inelegant squeak as he began to ascend toward the bedrooms. "This is really happening," she said, sounding slightly dazed.

"I thought you said you weren't drunk."

"I'm not."

"Then try not to look so surprised. It's making me question things. And I don't want to question things. I just want you."

She shivered in his hold. "You're not like most men I know."

"Pretty boys with popped collars and pastel polo shirts? I must be a real disappointment."

"Obviously you aren't. Obviously I don't care about men in pastel polo shirts or I would've gotten laid any number of times in the past decade."

He pushed open the bedroom door, threw her down over the simply appointed bed that was far too small for the kind of acrobatics he wanted to get up to tonight. Then he stood back, admiring her, wearing nothing but those half-open jeans riding low on her hips, her stomach dipping in with each breath, her breasts thrust into greater prominence at the same time.

"Were you waiting for me?" He kept the words light, taunting, because he knew that she liked it.

She had always liked sparring with him. That was what they'd always done. Of course she would like it now. Of course he would like it now. Or maybe it had nothing to do with her. Maybe it had everything to do with the fact that he had years' worth of dirty in him that needed to be let out.

"Screw you," she said, pushing herself back farther up the mattress so that her head was resting on the pillow. Then she put her hands behind her head, her blue gaze sharp. "Come on, cowboy. Get naked for me."

"Oh no, Maddy, you're not running the show."

"Ten years," she said, her gaze level with his. "Ten years, Sam. That's how long it's been since I've seen a naked man. And let me tell you, I have never seen a naked man like you." She held up a finger. "One man. One insipid man. He wasn't even that good."

"You haven't had sex for ten years and your last lover wasn't even good? I was sort of hoping that it had been so good you were waiting for your knees to stop shaking before you bothered to go out and get some again."

"If only. My knees never once shook. In fact,

they're shaking harder now and you haven't even gotten out of those pants yet."

"You give good dirty talk."

She lifted a shoulder. "I'm good at talking. That's about the thing I'm best at."

"Oh, I hope not, baby. I hope that mouth is good for a lot of other things too."

He saw her breasts hitch. Her eyes growing round. Then he smiled, grabbing hold of the hem of his shirt and stripping it off over his head. Her reaction was more satisfying than he could've possibly anticipated. It'd been a long time since he'd seen a woman looking at him that way.

Sure, women checked him out. That happened all the time. But this was different. This was raw, open hunger. She wasn't bothering to hide it. Why would she? They were both here to do this. No holds barred, no clothes, no nothing. Why bother to be coy? Why bother to pretend this was about anything other than satisfying lust. And if that was all it was, why should either of them bother to hide that lust.

"Keep looking at me like that, sweetheart, this is gonna end fast."

"Don't do that," she said, a wicked smile on her lips. "You're no good to me in that case."

"Don't worry, babe. I can get it up more than once."

At least, he could if he remembered correctly.

"Good thing I brought about three boxes of condoms."

"For two days? You did have high hopes for the weekend."

"Ten years," she reiterated.

"Point taken."

He moved his hands down, slowly working at his belt. The way that she licked her lips as her eyes followed his every movement ratcheting up his arousal another impossible notch.

Everything felt too sharp, too clear, every rasp of fabric over his skin, every downward flick of her eyes, every small, near-imperceptible gasp on her lips.

He hadn't been in a bedroom alone with a woman in a long damn time. And it was all catching up with him now.

Shutting down, being a mean bastard who didn't let anyone close? That was easy enough. It made it easy to forget. He shut the world out, stripped everything away. Reverted back to the way he had been just after his parents had died and it had been too difficult to feel anything more than his grief.

That was what he had done in the past five years. That was what he had done with his new, impossible loss that never should have happened. Wouldn't have if he'd had a shred of self-control and decency.

And now, tonight, he was proving that he probably still didn't have any at all. Oh well, just as well. Because he was going to do this.

He was going to do her.

He pushed his jeans down his lean hips, showing

her the extent of his desire for her, reveling in the
way her eyes widened when he revealed his body
completely to her hungry gaze.

"I have never seen one that big before," she said.

He laughed. "Are you just saying that because it's
what you think men need to hear?"

"No, I'm saying that because it's the biggest I've
ever seen. And I want it."

"Baby," he said, "you can have it."

Maddy turned over onto her stomach and crawled
across the bed on all fours in a move that damn near
gave him a heart attack. Then she moved to the edge
of the mattress, straightening up, raking her nails
down over his torso before she leaned in, flicking
her tongue over the head of his arousal.

He jerked beneath her touch, his length twitch-
ing as her tongue traced it from base to tip, just before she engulfed him completely in the warm heat
of her mouth. She hummed, the vibration moving
through his body, drawing his balls up tight. He really was going to lose it. Here and now like a green
teenage boy if he didn't get a grip on himself. Or a
grip on her.

He settled for the second option.

He reached back, grabbing hold of her hair and
jerking her lips away from him. "You keep doing
that and it really will end."

The color was high in her cheeks, her eyes glittering. "I've never, ever enjoyed it like that before."

She was so good for his ego. Way better than a

man like him deserved. But damned if he wasn't going to take it.

"Well, you can enjoy more of that. Later. Right now? I need to be inside you."

"Technically," she said, her tone one of protest, "you were inside me."

"And as much as I like being in that pretty mouth of yours, that isn't what I want right now." He gritted his teeth, looking around the room. "The condoms."

She scrambled off the bed and shimmied out of her jeans and panties as she made her way across the room and toward her suitcase. She flipped it open, dug through it frantically and produced the two packets he had seen earlier.

All things considered, he felt a little bit triumphant to be the one getting these condoms. He didn't know Christopher, but that sad sack was sitting at home with a hard-on, and Sam was having his woman. He was going to go ahead and enjoy the hell out of that.

Madison turned to face him, the sight of that enticing, pale triangle at the apex of her thighs sending a shot straight down to his gut. She kept her eyes on his as she moved nearer, holding one of the condoms like it was a reward he was about to receive.

She tore it open and settled back onto the bed, then leaned forward and rolled it over his length. Then she took her position back up against the pillows, her thighs parting, her heavily lidded gaze averted from his now that she was in that vulnerable position.

"Okay," she said, "I'm ready."

She wasn't. Not by a long shot.

Ten years.

And he had been ready to thrust into her with absolutely no finesse. A woman who'd been celibate for ten years deserved more than that. She deserved more than one orgasm. Hell, she deserved more than two.

He had never been the biggest fan of Madison West, but tonight they were allies. Allies in pleasure. And he was going to hold up his end of the bargain so well that if she was celibate after this, it really would be because she was waiting for her legs to work again.

"Not quite yet, Maddy," he said, kneeling down at the end of the bed, reaching forward and grabbing hold of her hips, dragging her down toward his face. He brought her up against his mouth, her legs thrown over his shoulders, that place where she was warm and wet for him right there, ready for him to taste her.

"Sam!" Maddy squeaked.

"There is no way you're a prude, Maddy," he said. "I've had too many conversations with you to believe that."

"I've never... No one has ever..."

"Then it's time somebody did."

He lowered his head, tasting her in long, slow

passes, like she was an ice-cream cone that he just had to take the time to savor. Like she was a delicacy he couldn't get enough of.

Because she was.

She was all warmth and sweet female, better than he had ever remembered a woman being. Or maybe she was just better. It was hard to say. He didn't really care which. It didn't matter. All that mattered was this.

If he could lose himself in any moment, in any time, it would be this one.

It sure as hell wouldn't be pounding iron, trying to hammer the guilt out of his body. Certainly wouldn't be in his damn sculptures, trying to figure out what to make next, trying to figure out how to satisfy the customer. This deeply personal thing that had started being given to the rest of the world, when he wasn't sure he wanted the rest of the world to see what was inside him.

Hell, *he* didn't want to see what was inside him.

He made a hell of a lot of money, carving himself out, making it into a product people could buy. And he sure as hell liked the money, but that didn't make it a pleasant experience.

No, none of that mattered. Not now. Not when there was Maddy. And that sweet sugar-whiskey taste.

He tasted her until she screamed, and then he thrust his fingers inside her, fast and rough, until he felt her pulse around him, until her orgasm swept through them both.

Then he moved up, his lips almost touching hers. "Now," he said, his voice husky, "now you're ready."

Four

Maddy was shaking from head to toe, and she honestly didn't know if she could take any more. She had never—not in her entire life—had an orgasm like that. It was still echoing through her body, creating little waves of sensation that shivered through her with each and every breath she took.

And there was still more. They weren't done. She was glad about that. She didn't want to be done. But at the same time she wasn't sure if she could handle the rest. But there he was, above her, over her, so hot and hard and male that she didn't think she could deny him. She didn't want to deny him.

She looked at him, at the broad expanse of his shoulders and chest, the way it tapered down to his narrow waist, those flat washboard abs that she could probably actually wash her clothes on.

He was everything a man should be. If the perfect fantasy man had been pulled straight out of her deepest fantasies, he would look like this. It hit her then that Christopher had not even been close to being a fantasy man. And that was maybe why he had been so safe. It was why Sam had always been so threatening.

Because Christopher had the power to make a ripple. Sam McCormack possessed the power to engulf her in a tidal wave.

She had no desire to be swept out to sea by any man. But in this instance she had a life preserver. And that was her general dislike of him. The fact that their time together was going to be contained to only this weekend. So what did it matter if she allowed herself to get a little bit storm tossed. It didn't. She was free. Free to enjoy this as much as she wanted.

And she wanted. *Wanted* with an endless hunger that seemed to growl inside her like a feral beast.

He possessed the equipment to satisfy it. She let her eyes drift lower than just his abs, taking in the heart, the unequivocal evidence, of his maleness. She had not been lying when she said it was the biggest one she'd ever seen. It made her feel a little bit intimidated. Especially since she had been celibate for so very long. But she had a few days to acclimate.

The thought made her giddy.

"Now," she said, not entirely certain that she was

totally prepared for him now but also unable to wait for him.

"You sure you're ready for me?" He leaned forward, bracing his hand on the headboard, poised over her like the very embodiment of carnal temptation. Just out of reach, close enough that she did easily inhale his masculine scent. Far enough away that he wasn't giving her what she needed. Not yet.

She felt hollow. Aching. And that, she realized, was how she knew she was going to take all of him whether or not it seemed possible. Because the only other option was remaining like this. Hollowed out and empty. And she couldn't stand that either. Not for one more second.

"Please," she said, not caring that she sounded plaintive. Not caring that she was begging. Begging Sam, the man she had spent the past several years harassing every time he came around her ranch.

No, she didn't care. She would make a fool out of herself if she had to, would lower herself as far down as she needed to go, if only she could get the kind of satisfaction that his body promised to deliver.

He moved his other hand up to the headboard, gripping it tight. Then he flexed his hips forward, the blunt head of his arousal teasing the slick entrance to her body. She reached up, bracing her palms flat against his chest, a shiver running through her as he teased her with near penetration.

She cursed. The sound quivering, weak in the near silence of the room. She had no idea where hard-ass

Maddy had gone. That tough, flippant girl who knew how to keep everyone at a distance with her words. Who knew how to play off every situation as if it weren't a big deal.

This was a big deal. How could she pretend that it wasn't? She was breaking apart from the inside out; how could she act as though she weren't?

"Please," she repeated.

He let go of the headboard with one hand and pressed his hand down next to her face, then repeated the motion with the other as he rocked his hips forward more fully, entering her slowly, inch by tantalizing inch. She gasped when he filled her all the way, the intense stretching sensation a pleasure more than it was a pain.

She slid her hands up to his shoulders, down his back, holding on to him tightly there before locking her legs around his lean hips and urging him even deeper.

"Yes," she breathed, a wave of satisfaction rolling over her, chased on the heels by a sense that she was still incomplete. That this wasn't enough. That it would never be enough.

Then he began to move. Ratcheting up the tension between them. Taking her need, her arousal, to greater heights than she had ever imagined possible. He was measured at first, taking care to establish a rhythm that helped her move closer to completion. But she didn't need the help. She didn't want it. She just wanted to ride the storm.

She tilted her head to the side, scraping her teeth along the tendon in his neck that stood out as a testament to his hard-won self-control.

And that did it.

He growled low in his throat. Then his movements became hard, harsh. Following no particular rhythm but his own. She loved it. Gloried in it. He grabbed hold of her hips, tugging her up against him every time he thrust down, making it rougher, making it deeper. Making it hurt. She felt full with it, full with him. This was exactly what she needed, and she hadn't even realized it. To be utterly and completely overwhelmed. To have this man consume her every sensation, her every breath.

She fused her lips to his, kissing him frantically as he continued to move inside her and she held on to him tighter, her nails digging into his skin. But she knew he didn't mind the pain. She knew it just as she didn't mind it. Knew it because he began to move harder, faster, reaching the edge of his own control as he pushed her nearer to the edge of hers.

Suddenly, it gripped her fiercely, down low inside her, a force of pleasure that she couldn't deny or control. She froze, stiffening against him, the scream that lodged itself in her throat the very opposite of who she usually was. It wasn't calculated; it wasn't pretty; it wasn't designed to do anything. It simply was. An expression of what she felt. Beyond her reach, beyond her completely.

She was racked with her desire for him, with the

intensity of the orgasm that swept through her. And then, just as she was beginning to find a way to breathe again, he found his own release, his hardness pulsing deep inside her as he gave himself up to it.

His release—the intensity of it—sent another shattering wave through her. And she clung to him even more tightly, needing him to anchor her to the bed, to the earth, or she would lose herself completely.

And then in the aftermath, she was left there, clinging to a stranger, having just shown the deepest, most hidden parts of herself to him. Having just lost her control with him in a way she never would have done with someone she knew better. Perhaps this was the only way she could have ever experienced this kind of freedom. The only way she could have ever let her guard down enough. What did she have to lose with Sam? His opinion of her was already low. So if he thought that she was a sex-hungry maniac after this, what did it matter?

He moved away from her and she threw her arm over her face, letting her head fall back, the sound of her fractured breathing echoing in the room.

After she had gulped in a few gasps of air, she removed her arm, opened her eyes and realized that Sam wasn't in the room anymore. Probably off to the bathroom to deal with necessities. Good. She needed some space. She needed a moment. At least a few breaths.

He returned a little bit quicker than she had hoped he might, all long lean muscle and satisfied male. It was the expression on his face that began to ease the tension in her chest. He didn't look angry. He didn't look like he was judging her. And he didn't look like he was in love with her or was about to start making promises that she didn't want him to make.

No, he just looked satisfied. A bone-deep satisfaction that she felt too.

"Holy hell," he said, coming to lie on the bed next to her, drawing her naked body up against his. She felt a smile curve her lips. "I think you about blew my head off."

"You're so romantic," she said, smiling even wider. Because this was perfect. Absolutely perfect.

"You don't want me to be romantic," he returned.

"No," she said, feeling happy, buoyant even. "I sure as hell don't."

"You want me to be bad, and dirty, and to be your every fantasy of slumming it with a man who is so very beneath you."

That, she took affront to a little bit. "I don't think you're beneath me, Sam," she said. Then he grabbed hold of her hips and lifted her up off the mattress before bringing her down over his body. A wicked smile crossed his face.

"I am now."

"You're insatiable. And terrible."

"For a weekend fling, honey, that's all you really need."

"Oh, dammit," she said, "what if the roads open up, and Christopher tries to come up?"

"I'm not really into threesomes." He tightened his grip on her. "And I'm not into sharing."

"No worries. I don't have any desire to broaden my experience by testing him out."

"Have I ruined you for him?"

The cocky bastard. She wanted to tell him no, but she had a feeling that denting the masculine ego when a man was underneath you wasn't the best idea if you wanted to have sex with said man again.

"Ruined me completely," she responded. "In fact, I should leave a message for him."

Sam snagged the phone on the nightstand and thrust it at her. "You can leave him a message now."

"Okay," she said, grimacing slightly.

She picked up the phone and dialed Christopher's number quickly. Praying that she got his voice mail and not his actual voice.

Of course, if she did, that meant he'd gone out. Which meant that maybe he was trying to find sex to replace the sex that he'd lost. Which she had done; she couldn't really be annoyed about that. But she had baggage.

"Come on," she muttered as the phone rang endlessly. Then she breathed a sigh of relief when she got his voice mail. "Hi, Christopher, it's Madison. Don't worry about coming up here if the roads clear up. If that happens, I'm probably just going to go back to Copper Ridge. The weekend is kind of ruined. And…and maybe you should just wait for me to call you?" She looked up at Sam, who was nearly vibrating with forcibly contained laughter. She rolled her eyes. "Anyway, sorry that this didn't work out. Bye."

"That was terrible," he said. "But I think you made it pretty clear that you don't want to hear from him."

"I said I would call him," she said in protestation.

"Are you going to?"

"*Hell* no."

Sam chuckled, rolling her back underneath him, kissing her deep, hard. "Good thing I only want a weekend."

"Why is that?"

"God help the man that wants more from you."

"Oh, please, that's not fair." She wiggled, luxuriating in the hard feel of him between her thighs. He wanted her again already. "I pity the woman that falls for you, Sam McCormack."

A shadow passed over his face. "So do I."

Then, as quickly as they had appeared, those clouds cleared and he was smiling again, that wicked, intense smile that let her know he was about ready to take her to heaven again.

"It's a good thing both of us only want a weekend."

Five

"How did the art retreat go?"

Sam gritted his teeth against his younger brother's questioning as Chase walked into their workshop. "Fine," he returned.

"Fine?" Chase leaned against the doorframe, crossing his arms, looking a little too much like Sam for his own comfort. Because he was a bastard, and he didn't want to see his bastard face looking back at him. "I thought you were going to get inspiration. To come up with the ideas that will keep the McCormack Ranch flush for the next several years."

"I'm not a machine," Sam said, keeping his tone hard. "You can't force art."

He said things like that, in that tone, because he

knew that no one would believe that cliché phrase, even if it was true. He didn't like that it was true.

But there wasn't much he was willing to do about it either.

"Sure. And I feel a slight amount of guilt over pressuring you, but since I do a lot of managing of your career, I consider it a part of my job."

"Stick to pounding iron, Chase—that's where your talents lie."

"I don't have talent," Chase said. "I have business sense. Which you don't have. So you should be thankful for me."

"You say that. You say it a lot. I think mostly because you know that I actually shouldn't be all that thankful for your meddling."

He was being irritable, and he knew it. But he didn't want Chase asking how the weekend was. He didn't want to explain the way he had spent his time. And he really didn't want to get into why the only thing he was inspired to do was start painting nudes.

Of one woman in particular.

Because the only kind of grand inspirational moments he'd had were when he was inside Maddy. Yeah, he wasn't going to explain that to his younger brother. He was never going to tell anybody. And he had to get his shit together.

"Seriously, though, everything is going okay? Anna is worried about you."

"Your wife is meddlesome. I liked her better when she was just your friend and all she did was come by for pizza a couple times a week. And she didn't worry too much about what I was doing or whether or not I was happy."

"Yeah, sadly for you she has decided she loves me. And by extension she has decided she loves you, which means her getting up in your business. I don't think she knows another way to be."

"Tell her to go pull apart a tractor and stop digging around in my life."

"No, thanks, I like my balls where they are. Which means I will not be telling Anna what to do. Ever."

"I liked it better when you were miserable and alone."

Chase laughed. "Why, because you're miserable and alone?"

"No, that would imply that I'm uncomfortable with the state of things. I myself am quite dedicated to my solitude and my misery."

"They say misery loves company," Chase said.

"Only true if you aren't a hermit."

"I suppose that's true." His brother looked at him, his gaze far too perceptive for Sam's liking. "You didn't used to be this terrible."

"I have been for a while." But worse with Maddy. She pushed at him. At things and needs and desires that were best left in the past.

He gritted his teeth. She pushed at him because he turned her on and that made her mad. He... Well, it was complicated.

"Yes," Chase said. "For a while."

"Don't psychoanalyze me. Maybe it's a crazy artist thing. Dad always said that it would make me a pussy."

"You aren't a pussy. You're a jerk."

"Six of one, half dozen of the other. Either way, I have issues."

Chase shook his head. "Well, deal with them on your own time. You have to be over at the West Ranch in less than an hour." Chase shook his head. "Pretty soon we'll be released from the contract. But you know until then we could always hire somebody else to go. You don't have to do horseshoes if you don't want. We're kind of beyond that now."

Sam gritted his teeth. For the first time he was actually tempted to take his brother up on the offer. To replace his position with someone else. Mostly because the idea of seeing Madison again filled him with the kind of reckless tension that he knew he wouldn't be able to do anything about once he saw her again.

Oh, not because of her. Not because of anything to do with her moral code or protestations. He could demolish those easily enough. It was because he couldn't afford to waste any more time thinking about her. Because he couldn't afford to get in any deeper. What had happened over the past weekend had been good. Damn good. But he had to leave it there.

Normally, he relished the idea of getting in there

and doing grunt work. There was something about it that fulfilled him. Chase might not understand that.

But Sam wasn't a paperwork man. He wasn't a business mind. He needed physical exertion to keep himself going.

His lips twitched as he thought about the kind of physical exertion he had indulged in with Maddy. Yeah, it kind of all made sense. Why he had thrown himself into the blacksmithing thing during his celibacy. He needed to pound something, one way or another. And since he had been so intent on denying himself female companionship, he had picked up a hammer instead.

He was tempted to back out. To make sure he kept his distance from Maddy. He wouldn't, because he was also far too tempted to go. Too tempted to test his control and see if there was a weak link. If he might end up with her underneath him again.

It would be the better thing to send Chase. Or to call in and say they would have to reschedule, then hire somebody else to take over that kind of work. They could more than afford it. But as much as he wanted to avoid Maddy, he wanted to see her again.

Just because.

His body began to harden just thinking about it.

"It's fine. I'm going to head over. You know that I like physical labor."

"I just don't understand why," Chase said, looking genuinely mystified.

But hell, Chase had a life. A wife. Things that

Sam was never going to have. Chase had worked through his stuff and made them both a hell of a lot of money, and Sam was happy for him. As happy as he ever got.

"You don't need to understand me. You just have to keep me organized so that I don't end up out on the street."

"You would never end up out on the streets of Copper Ridge. Mostly because if you stood out there with a cardboard sign, some well-meaning elderly woman would wrap you in a blanket and take you back to her house for casserole. And you would rather die. We both know that."

That made Sam smile reluctantly. "True enough."

"So, I guess you better keep working, then."

Sam thought about Maddy again, about her sweet, supple curves. About how seeing her again was going to test him in the best way possible. Perhaps that was why he should go. Just so he could test himself. Push up against his control. Yeah, maybe that was what he needed.

Yeah, that justification worked well. And it meant he would see her again.

It wasn't feelings. It was just sex. And he was starting to think just sex might be what he needed.

"I plan on it."

Maddy took a deep breath of clean salt air and arena dirt. There was something comforting about it. Familiar. Whenever things had gone wrong in her life, this was what she could count on. The familiar sights and sounds of the ranch, her horses. Herself.

She never felt stronger than when she was on the back of a horse, working in time with the animal to move from a trot to a walk, a walk to a halt. She never felt more understood.

A funny thing. Because, while she knew she was an excellent trainer and she had full confidence in her ability to keep control over the animal, she knew that she would never have absolute control. Animals were unpredictable. Always.

One day, they could simply decide they didn't want to deal with you and buck you off. It was the risk that every person who worked with large beasts took. And they took it on gladly.

She liked that juxtaposition. The control, the danger. The fact that though she achieved a certain level of mastery with each horse she worked with, they could still decide they weren't going to behave on a given day.

She had never felt much of that in the rest of her life. Often she felt like she was fighting against so much. Having something like this, something that made her feel both small and powerful had been essential to her well-being. Especially during all that crap that had happened ten years ago. She had been thinking more about it lately. Honestly, it had all started because of Christopher, because she had been considering breaking her celibacy. And it had only gotten worse after she actually had. After Sam.

Mostly because she couldn't stop thinking about him. Mostly because she felt like one weekend could never be enough. And she needed it to be. She badly needed it to be. She needed to be able to have sex with a guy without having lingering feelings for him. David had really done a number on her, and she did not want another number done on her.

It was for the best if she never saw Sam again. She knew that was unlikely, but it would be better. She let out a deep breath, walking into the barn, her riding boots making a strident sound on the hard-packed dirt as she walked in. Then she saw movement toward the end of the barn, someone coming out of one of the stalls.

She froze. It wasn't uncommon for there to be other people around. Her family employed a full staff to keep the ranch running smoothly, but for some reason this felt different. And a couple of seconds later, as the person came into view, she realized why.

Black cowboy hat, broad shoulders, muscular forearms. That lean waist and hips. That built, muscular physique that she was intimately acquainted with.

Dear Lord. Sam McCormack was here.

She had known that there would be some compromise on the never-seeing-him-again thing; she had just hoped that it wouldn't be seeing him now.

"Sam," she said, because she would be damned if she appeared like she had been caught unawares. "I didn't expect you to be here."

"Your father wanted to make sure that all of the horses were in good shape before the holidays, since it was going to delay my next visit."

Maddy gritted her teeth. Christmas was in a couple of weeks, which meant her family would be having their annual party. The festivities had started to become a bit threadbare and brittle in recent years. Now that everybody knew Nathan West had been forced to sell off all of his properties downtown. Now that everyone knew he had a bastard son, Jack Monaghan, whose existence Nathan had tried to deny for more than thirty years. Yes, now that everybody had seen the cracks in the gleaming West family foundation, it all seemed farcical to Maddy.

But then, seeing as she had been one of the first major cracks in the foundation, she supposed that she wasn't really entitled to be too judgmental about it. However, she was starting to feel a bit exhausted.

"Right," she returned, knowing that her voice sounded dull.

"Have you seen Christopher?"

His question caught her off guard, as did his tone, which sounded a bit hard and possessive. It was funny, because this taciturn man in front of her was more what she had considered Sam to be before they had spent those days in the cabin together. Those days—where they had mostly been naked—had been a lot easier. Quieter. He had smiled more. But then, she supposed that any man receiving an endless supply of orgasms was prone to smiling more. They had barely gotten out of bed.

They had both been more than a little bit insatiable, and Maddy hadn't minded that at all. But this was a harsh slap back to reality. To a time that could almost have been before their little rendezvous but clearly wasn't, because his line of questioning was tinged with jealousy.

"No. As you guessed, I lied to him and didn't call him."

"And he call you?"

Maddy lifted her fingernail and began to chew on it, grimacing when she realized she had just ruined her manicure. "He did call," she said, her face heating slightly. "And I changed his name in my phone book to Don't Answer."

"Why did you do that?"

"Obviously you can't delete somebody from your phone book when you don't want to talk to them, Sam. You have to make sure that you know who's calling. But I like the reminder that I'm not speaking to him. Because then my phone rings and the screen says Don't Answer, and then I go, 'Okay.'"

"I really do pity the man who ends up wanting to chase after you."

"Good thing you don't. Except, oh wait, you're here."

She regretted that as soon as she said it. His gaze darkened, his eyes sweeping over her figure. Why did she want to push him?

Why did she always want to push him?

"You know why I'm here."

"Yes, because my daddy pays you to be here." She didn't know why she said that. To reinforce the difference between them? To remind him she was Lady of the Manor, and that regardless of his bank balance he was socially beneath her? To make herself look like a stupid rich girl he wouldn't want to mess around with anyway. Honestly, these days it was difficult for her to guess at her own motives.

"Is this all part of your fantasy? You want to be… taken by the stable boy or something? I mean, it's a nice one, Maddy, and I didn't really mind acting it out with you last weekend, but we both know that I'm not exactly the stable boy and you're not exactly the breathless virgin."

Heat streaked through her face, rage pooling in her stomach. "Right. Because I'm not some pure, snow-white virgin, my fantasies are somehow wrong?" It was too close to that wound. The one she wished wasn't there. The one she couldn't ignore, no matter how much she tried.

"That wasn't the point I was making. And anyway, when your whole fantasy about a man centers around him being bad for you, I'm not exactly sure where you get off trying to take the moral-outrage route."

"I will be as morally outraged as I please," she snapped, turning to walk away from him.

He reached out, grabbing hold of her arm and

turning her back to face him, taking hold of her other arm and pulling her forward. "Everything was supposed to stay back up at those cabins," he said, his voice rough.

"So why aren't you letting it?" she spat. Reckless. Shaky. She was a hypocrite. Because she wasn't letting it rest either.

"Because you walked in in those tight pants and it made it a lot harder for me to think."

"My breeches," she said, keeping the words sharp and crisp as a green apple, "are not typically the sort of garment that inspire men to fits of uncontrollable lust." Except *she* was drowning in a fit of uncontrollable lust. His gaze was hot, his hands on her arms even hotter. She wanted to arch against him, to press her breasts against his chest as she had done more times than she could count when they had been together. She wanted… She wanted the impossible. She wanted more. More of him. More of everything they had shared together, even though they had agreed that would be a bad idea.

Even though she knew it was something she shouldn't even want.

"Your pretty little ass in anything would make a man lose his mind. Don't tell me those breeches put any man off, or I'm gonna have to call you a liar."

"It isn't my breeches that put them off. That's just my personality."

"If some man can't handle you being a little bit hard, then he's no kind of man. I can take you, baby.

I can take all of you. And that's good, since we both know you can take all of me."

"Are you just going to be a tease, Sam?" she asked, echoing back a phrase that had been uttered to her by many men over the years. "Or is this leading somewhere?"

"You don't want it to lead anywhere, you said so yourself." He released his hold on her, taking a step back.

"You're contrary, Sam McCormack—do you know that?"

He laughed. "That's about the only thing anyone calls me. We both know what I am. The only thing that confuses me is exactly why you seem surprised by it now."

She was kind of stumped by that question. Because really, the only answer was sex. That she had imagined that the two of them being together, that the man he had been during that time, meant something.

Which proved that she really hadn't learned anything about sexual relationships, in spite of the fact that she had been so badly wounded by one in the past. She had always known that she had a hard head, but really, this was ridiculous.

But it wasn't just her head that was hard. She had hardened up a considerable amount in the years since her relationship with David. Because she'd had to. Because within the equestrian community, she had spent the years following that affair known as the skank who had seriously jeopardized the marriage of an upright member of the community. Never mind that she had been his student. Never mind that she had been seventeen years old, a virgin who had believed every word that had come out of the esteemed older man's mouth. Who had believed that his marriage really was over and that he wanted a life and a future with her.

It was laughable to her now. Any man nearing his forties who found himself able to relate to a seventeen-year-old on an emotional level was a little bit suspect. A married one, in a position of power, was even worse. She knew all of that. She knew it down to her bones. Believing it was another thing.

So sometimes her judgment was in doubt. Sometimes she felt like an idiot. But she was much more equipped to deal with difficult situations now. She was a lot pricklier. A lot more inured.

And that was what came to her defense now.

"Sam, if you still want me, all you have to do is say it. Don't you stand there growling because you're hard and sexually frustrated and we both agreed that it would only be that one weekend. Just be a man and admit it."

"Are you sure you should be talking to me like that here? Anyone can catch us. If I backed you up against that wall and kissed your smart mouth, then people would know. Doesn't it make you feel dirty? Doesn't it make you feel ashamed?" His words lashed at her, made her feel all of those things but also aroused her. She had no idea what was wrong with her. Except that maybe part of it was that she simply didn't know how to feel desire without feeling ashamed. Another gift from her one and only love affair.

"You're the one that's saying all of this. Not me," she said, keeping her voice steely. She lifted a shoulder. "If I didn't know better, I would say you have issues. I don't want to help you work those out." A sudden rush of heat took over, a reckless thought that she had no business having, that she really should work to get a handle on. But she didn't.

She took a deep breath. "I don't have any desire to help you with your issues, but if you're horny, I can help you with that."

"What the hell?"

"You heard me," she said, crossing her arms and giving him her toughest air. "If you want me, then have me."

Sam could hardly believe what he was hearing. Yet again, Madison West was propositioning him. And this time, he was pissed off. Because he wasn't a dog that she could bring to heel whenever she wanted to. He wasn't the kind of man who could be manipulated.

Even worse, he wanted her. He wanted to say yes. And he wasn't sure he could spite his dick to soothe his pride.

"You can't just come in here and start playing games with me," he said. "I'm not a dog that you can call whenever you want me to come."

He let the double meaning of that statement sit between them. "That isn't what I'm doing," she said, her tone waspish.

"Then what are you doing, Madison? We agreed that it would be one weekend. And then you come in here sniping at me, and suddenly you're propositioning me. I gave in to all of this when you asked the first time, because I'm a man. And I'm not going to say no in a situation like the one we were in. But I'm also not the kind of man you can manipulate."

Color rose high in her cheeks. "I'm not trying to manipulate you. Why is it that men are always accusing me of that?"

"Because no man likes to be turned on and then left waiting," he returned.

The color in her cheeks darkened, and then she turned on one boot heel and walked quickly away from him.

He moved after her, reaching out and grabbing hold of her arm, stopping her. "What? Now you're going to go?"

"I can't do this. I can't do this if you're going to wrap all of it up in accusations and shame. I've been there. I've done it, Sam, and I'm not doing it again. Trust me. I've been accused of a lot of things. I've had my fill of it. So, great, you don't want to be manipulated. I don't want to be the one that has to leave this affair feeling guilty."

Sam frowned. "That's not what I meant."

She was the one who was being unreasonable,

blowing hot and cold on him. How was it that he had been the one to be made to feel guilty? He didn't like that. He didn't like feeling anything but irritation and desire for her. He certainly didn't want to feel any guilt.

He didn't want to feel any damn thing.

"Well, what did you mean? Am I a tease, Sam? Is that what I am? And men like you just can't help themselves?"

He took a step back. "No," he said. "But you do have to make a decision. Either you want this, or you don't."

"Or?"

"Or nothing," he said, his tone hard. "If you don't want it, you don't want it. I'm not going to coerce you into anything. But I don't do the hot-and-cold thing."

Of course, he didn't really do any kind of thing anymore. But this, this back and forth, reminded him too much of his interaction with Elizabeth. Actually, all of it reminded him a little bit too much of Elizabeth. This seemingly soft, sweet woman with a bit of an edge. Someone who was high-class and a little bit luxurious. Who felt like a break from his life on the ranch. His life of rough work and solitude.

But after too much back and forth, it had ended. And he didn't speak to her for months. Until he had gotten a call that he needed to go to the hospital.

He gritted his teeth, looking at Madison. He couldn't imagine anything with Madison ending quite that way, not simply because he refused to ever lose his control the way he had done with Elizabeth, but also because he couldn't imagine Maddy slinking off in silence. She might go hot and cold, but she would never do it quietly.

"Twelve days. There are twelve days until Christmas. That's what I want. Twelve days to get myself on the naughty list. So to speak." She leveled her blue gaze with his. "If you don't want to oblige me, I'm sure Christopher will. But I would much rather it be you."

"Why?" He might want this, but he would be damned if he would make it easy for her. Mostly because he wanted to make it a little harder on himself.

"Because I planned to go up to that cabin and have sex with Christopher. I had to, like, come up with a plan. A series of tactical maneuvers that would help me make the decision to get it over with after all that time. You," she said, gesturing at him, "you, I didn't plan to have anything happen with. Ever. But I couldn't stop myself. I think at the end of the day it's much better to carry on a sex-only affair with a man that you can't control yourself with. Like right now. I was not going to proposition you today, Sam. I promise. Not today, not ever again. In fact, I'm mad at you, so it should be really easy for me to walk away. But I don't want to. I want you. I want you even if it's a terrible idea."

He looked around, then took her arm again, dragging her into one of the empty stalls, where they would be out of sight if anyone walked into the barn.

Then he pressed her against the wall, gripping her chin and taking her mouth in a deep, searing kiss. She whimpered, arching against him, grabbing hold of his shoulders and widening her stance so that he could press his hardened length against where she was soft and sensitive, ready for him already.

He slid his hand down her back, not caring that the hard wall bit into his knuckles as he grabbed hold of her rear, barely covered by those riding pants, which ought to have been illegal.

She whimpered, wiggling against him, obviously trying to get some satisfaction for the ache inside her. He knew that she felt it, because he felt the same way. He wrenched his mouth away from hers. "Dammit," he said, "I have to get back to work."

"Do you really?" She looked up at him, her expression so desperate it was nearly comical. Except he felt too desperate to laugh.

"Yes," he said.

"Well, since my family owns the property, I feel like I can give you permission to—"

He held up a hand. "I'm going to stop you right there. Nobody gives me permission to do anything. If I didn't want to finish the day's work, I wouldn't. I don't need the money. That's not why I do this. It's my reputation. My pride. I'm contracted to do it, and I will do what I promised I would. But when the contract is up? I won't."

"Oh," she said. "I didn't realize that."

"Everything is going well with the art business."

At least, it would if he could think of something else to do. He supposed he could always do more animals and cowboys. People never got tired of that. They had been his most popular art installations so far.

"Great. That's great. Maybe you could…not press yourself up against me? Because I'm going to do something really stupid in a minute."

He did not comply with her request; instead, he kept her there, held up against the wall. "What's that?"

She frowned. "Something I shouldn't do in a public place."

"You're not exactly enticing me to let you go." His body was so hard he was pretty sure he was going to turn to stone.

"I'll bite you."

"Still not enticed."

"Are you telling me that you want to get bitten?"

He rolled his hips forward, let her feel exactly what she was doing to him. "Biting can be all part of the fun."

"I have some things to learn," she said, her blue eyes widening.

"I'm happy to teach them to you," he said, wavering on whether or not he would finish what they'd started here. "Where should I meet you tonight?"

"Here," she said, the word rushed.

"Are you sure? I live on the same property as Chase, but in different houses. We are close, but not that close."

"No, I have my own place here too. And there's always a lot of cars. It won't look weird. I just don't want anyone to see me…" She looked away from him. "I don't want to advertise."

"That's fine." It suited him to keep everyone in the dark too. He didn't want the kind of attention that would come with being associated with Madison West. Already, the attention that he got for the various art projects he did, for the different displays around town, was a little much for him.

It was an impossible situation for him, as always. He wanted things that seemed destined to require more of himself than he wanted to give. Things that seemed to need him to reach deep, when it was better if he never did. Yet he seemed to choose them. Women like Madison. A career like art.

Someday he would examine that. Not today.

"Okay," she said, "come over after it's dark."

"This is like a covert operation."

"Is that a problem?"

It really wasn't. It was hypocritical of him to pretend otherwise. Hell, his last relationship—the one with Elizabeth—had been conducted almost entirely in secrecy because he had been going out of town to see her. That had been her choice, because she knew her association with him would be an issue for her family.

And, as he already established, he didn't really want anyone to know about this thing with Maddy either. Still, sneaking around felt contrary to his nature too. In general, he didn't really care what people thought about him. Or about his decisions.

You're a liar.

He gritted his teeth. Everything with Elizabeth was its own exception. There was no point talking to anyone about it. No point getting into that terrible thing he had been a part of. The terrible thing he had caused.

"Not a problem," he said. "I'll see you in a few hours."

"I can cook," she said as he turned to walk out of the stall.

"You don't have to. I can grab something on my way."

"No, I would rather we had dinner."

He frowned. "Maddy," he began, "this isn't going to be a relationship. It can't be."

"I know," she said, looking up and away from him, swallowing hard. "But I need for it to be something a little more than just sex too. I just... Look, obviously you know that somebody that hasn't had a sexual partner in the past ten years has some baggage. I do. Shocking, I know, because I seem like a bastion of mental health. But I just don't like the feeling. I really don't."

His chest tightened. Part of him was tempted to ask her exactly what had happened. Why she had been celibate for so long. But then, if they began to trade stories about their pasts, she might want to know something about his. And he wasn't getting into that. Not now, not ever.

"Is there anything you don't like?"

"No," he said, "I'm easy. I thought you said you didn't cook?"

She shrugged a shoulder. "Okay, if I'm being completely honest, I have a set of frozen meals in my freezer that my parents' housekeeper makes for me. But I can heat up a double portion so we can eat together."

He shook his head. "Okay."

"I have pot roast, meat loaf and roast chicken."

"I'll tell you what. The only thing I want is to have your body for dessert. I'll let you go ahead and plan dinner."

"Pot roast it is," she said, her voice a borderline squeak.

He chuckled, turning and walking away from her, something shifting in his chest. He didn't know how she managed to do that. Make him feel heavier one moment, then lighter the next. It was dangerous. That's what it was. And if he had a brain in his head, he would walk away from her and never look back.

Sadly, his ability to think with his brain had long since ceased to function.

Even if it was a stupid idea, and he was fairly certain it was, he was going to come to Madison's house tonight, and he was going to have her in about every way he could think of.

He fixed his mouth into a grim line and set about

finishing his work. But while he kept his face completely stoic, inside he felt anticipation for the first time in longer than he could remember.

Six

Maddy wondered if seductresses typically wore pearls. Probably pearls and nothing else. Maybe pearls and lace. Probably not high-waisted pencil skirts and cropped sweaters. But warming pot roast for Sam had put her in the mind-set of a 1950s housewife, and she had decided to go ahead and embrace the theme.

She caught a glimpse of her reflection in the mirror in the hall of her little house and she laughed at herself. She was wearing red lipstick, her blond hair pulled back into a bun. She rolled her eyes, then stuck out her tongue. Then continued on into the kitchen, her high heels clicking on the tile.

At least underneath the sweater, she had on a piece of pretty hot lingerie, if she said so herself. She knew

Sam was big on the idea that seduction couldn't be planned, but Maddy did like to have a plan. It helped her feel more in control, and when it came to Sam, she had never felt more out of control.

She sighed, reaching up into the cupboard and taking out a bottle of wine that she had picked up at Grassroots Winery that afternoon. She might not be the best cook, or any kind of cook at all, but she knew how to pick a good wine. Everyone had their strengths.

The strange thing was she kind of enjoyed feeling out of control with Sam, but it also made her feel cautious. Protective. When she had met David, she had dived into the affair headlong. She hadn't thought at all. She had led entirely with her heart, and in the end, she had gotten her heart broken. More than that, the aftermath had shattered her entire world. She had lost friends; she had lost her standing within a community that had become dear to her… Everything.

"But you aren't seventeen. And Sam isn't a married douche bag." She spoke the words fiercely into the silence of the kitchen, buoyed by the reality of them.

She could lose a little bit of control with Sam. Even within that, there would be all of her years, her wisdom—such as it was—and her experience. She was never going to be the girl she had been. That was a good thing. She would never be able to be hurt like that, not again. She simply didn't possess the emotional capacity.

She had emerged Teflon coated. Everything slid off now.

There was a knock on her front door and she straightened, closing her eyes and taking a deep breath, trying to calm the fluttering in her stomach. That reminded her a bit too much of the past. Feeling all fluttery and breathless just because she was going to see the man she was fixated on. That felt a little too much like emotion.

No. It wasn't emotion. It was just anticipation. She was old enough now to tell the difference between the two things.

She went quickly to the door, suddenly feeling a little bit ridiculous as she pulled it open. When it was too late for her to do anything about it. Her feeling of ridiculousness only increased when she saw Sam standing there, wearing his typical black cowboy hat, tight T-shirt and well-fitted jeans. Of course, he didn't need to wear anything different to be hotter to her.

A cowboy hat would do it every time.

"Hi," she said, taking a step back and gesturing with her hand. "Come in."

He obliged, walking over the threshold and looking around the space. For some reason, she found herself looking at it through his eyes. Wondering what kinds of conclusions he would draw about the neat, spare environment.

She had lived out in the little guesthouse ever since she was nineteen. Needing a little bit of distance from her family but never exactly leaving. For the first time, that seemed a little bit weird to her. It had always just been her life. She worked on the ranch, so there didn't seem to be any point in leaving it.

Now she tried to imagine explaining it to someone else—to Sam—and she wondered if it was weird.

"My mother's interior decorator did the place," she said. "Except for the yellow and red." She had added little pops of color through throw pillows, vases and art on the wall. But otherwise the surroundings were predominantly white.

"Great," he said, clearly not interested at all.

It had felt weird, thinking about him judging her based on the space, thinking about him judging her circumstances. But it was even weirder to see that he wasn't even curious.

She supposed that was de rigueur for physical affairs. And that was what this was.

"Dinner is almost ready," she said, reminding them both of the nonphysical part of the evening. Now she felt ridiculous for suggesting that too. But the idea of meeting him in secret had reminded her way too much of David. Somehow, adding pot roast had seemed to make the whole thing aboveboard.

Pot roast was an extremely nonsalacious food.

"Great," he said, looking very much like he didn't actually care that much.

"I just have to get it out of the microwave." She treated him to an exaggerated wink.

That earned her an uneasy laugh. "Great," he said.

"Come on," she said, gesturing for him to follow her. She moved into the kitchen, grabbed the pan that contained the meat and the vegetables out of the microwave and set it on the table, where the place settings were already laid out and the salad was already waiting.

"I promise I'm not trying to Stepford-wife you," she said as they both took their seats.

"I didn't think that," he said, but his blank expression betrayed the fact that he was lying.

"You did," she said. "You thought that I was trying to become your creepy robot wife."

"No, but I did wonder exactly why dinner was so important."

She looked down. It wasn't as if David were a secret. In fact, the affair was basically open information. "Do you really want to know?"

Judging by the expression on his face, he didn't. "There isn't really a good way to answer that question."

"True. Honesty is probably not the best policy. I'll think you're uninterested in me."

"On the contrary, I'm very interested in you."

"Being interested in my boobs is not the same thing."

He laughed, taking a portion of pot roast out of the dish in the center of the table. "I'm going to eat. If you want to tell me...well, go ahead. But I don't think you're trying to ensnare me."

"You don't?"

"Honestly, Maddy, nobody would want me for that long."

Those words were spoken with a bit of humor, but they made her sad. "I'm sure that's not true," she said, even though she wasn't sure of any such thing. He was grumpy. And he wasn't the most adept emotionally. Still, it didn't seem like a very kind thing for a person to think about themselves.

"It is," he said. "Chase is only with me because he's stuck with me. He feels some kind of loyalty to our parents."

"I thought your parents…"

"They're dead," he responded, his tone flat.

"I'm sorry," she said.

"Me too."

Silence fell between them after that, and she knew the only way to break it was to go ahead and get it out. "The first guy…the one ten years ago, we were having a physical-only affair. Except I didn't know it."

"Ouch," Sam said.

"Very. I mean, trust me, there were plenty of signs. And even though he was outright lying to me about his intentions, if I had been a little bit older or more experienced, I would have known. It's a terrible thing to find out you're a cliché. I imagine you wouldn't know what that's like."

"No, not exactly. Artist-cowboy-blacksmith is not really a well-worn template."

She laughed and took a sip of her wine. "No, I

guess not." Then she took another sip. She needed something to fortify her. Anything.

"But other woman that actually believes he'll leave his wife for you, that is." She swallowed hard, waiting for his face to change, waiting for him to call her a name, to get disgusted and walk out.

It occurred to her just then that that was why she was telling him all of this. Because she needed him to know. She needed him to know, and she needed to see what he would think. If he would still want her. Or if he would think that she was guilty beyond forgiving.

There were a lot of people who did.

But he didn't say anything. And his face didn't change. So they just sat in silence for a moment.

"When we got involved, he told me that he was done with her. That their marriage was a mess and they were already starting divorce proceedings. He said that he just wore his wedding ring to avoid awkward questions from their friends. The dressage community around here is pretty small, and he said that he and his wife were waiting until they could tell people themselves, personally, so that there were no rumors flying around." She laughed, almost because she was unable to help it. It was so ridiculous. She wanted to go back and shake seventeen-year-old her. For being such an idiot. For caring so much.

"Anyway," she continued, "he said he wanted to protect me. You know, because of how unkind people can be."

"He was married," Sam said.

She braced herself. "Yes," she returned, unflinching.

"How old were you?"

"Seventeen."

"How old was he?"

"Almost forty."

Sam cursed. "He should have been arrested."

"Maybe," she said, "except I did want him."

She had loved the attention he had given her. Had loved feeling special. It had been more than lust. It had been neediness. For all the approval she hadn't gotten in her life. Classic daddy issues, basically. But, as messed up as a man his age had to be for wanting to fool around with a teenager, the teenager had to be pretty screwed up too.

"How did you know him?"

"He was my... He was my trainer."

"Right, so some jackass in a position of power. Very surprising."

Warmth bloomed in her chest and spread outward, a strange, completely unfamiliar sensation. There were only a few people on earth who defended her when the subject came up. And mostly, they kept it from coming up. Sierra, her younger sister, knew about it only from the perspective of someone who had been younger at the time. Maddy had shared a little bit about it, about the breakup and how much it had messed with her, when Sierra was having difficulty in her own love life.

And then there were her brothers, Colton and

Gage. Who would both have cheerfully killed David if they had ever been able to get their hands on him. But Sam was the first person she had ever told the whole story to. And he was the first person who wasn't one of her siblings who had jumped to her defense immediately.

There had been no interrogation about what kinds of clothes she'd worn to her lessons. About how she had behaved. Part of her wanted to revel in it. Another part of her wanted to push back at it.

"Well, I wore those breeches around him. I know they made you act a little bit crazy. Maybe it was my fault."

"Is this why you got mad about what I said earlier?"

She lifted a shoulder. "Well, that and it was mean."

"I didn't realize this had happened to you," he said, his voice not exactly tender but full of a whole lot more sympathy than she had ever imagined getting from him. "I'm sorry."

"The worst part was losing all my friends," she said, looking up at him. "Everybody really liked him. He was their favorite instructor. As far as dressage instructors go, he was young and cool, trust me."

"So you bore the brunt of it because he turned out to be human garbage and nobody wanted to face it?"

The way he phrased that, so matter-of-fact and real, made a bubble of humor well up inside her chest. "I guess so."

"That doesn't seem fair."

"It really doesn't."

"So that's why you had to feed me dinner, huh? So I didn't remind you of that guy?"

"Well, you're nothing like him. For starters, he was…much more diminutive."

Sam laughed. "You make it sound like you had an affair with a leprechaun."

"Jockeys aren't brawny, Sam."

He only laughed harder. "That's true. I suppose that causes trouble with wind resistance and things."

She rolled her eyes. "You are terrible. Obviously he had some appeal." Though, she had a feeling it wasn't entirely physical. Seeing as she had basically been seeking attention and approval and a thousand other things besides orgasms.

"Obviously. It was his breeches," Sam said.

"A good-looking man in breeches is a thing."

"I believe you."

"But a good-looking man in Wranglers is better." At least, that was her way of thinking right at the moment.

"Good to know."

"But you can see. Why I don't really want to advertise this. It has nothing to do with what you do or who you are or who I am. Well, I guess it is all to do with who I am. What people already think about me. I've been completely defined by a sex life I barely have. And that was… It was the smallest part of that betrayal. At least for me. I loved him. And he was just using me."

"I hope his life was hell after."

"No. His wife forgave him. He went on to compete in the Olympics. He won a silver medal."

"That's kind of a karmic letdown."

"You're telling me. Meanwhile, I've basically lived like a nun and continued giving riding lessons here on the family ranch. I didn't go on to do any of the competing that I wanted to, because I couldn't throw a rock without hitting a judge who was going to be angry with me for my involvement with David."

"In my opinion," Sam said, his expression turning dark, focused, "people are far too concerned with who women sleep with and not near enough as concerned as they should be about whether or not the man does it well. Was he good?"

She felt her face heat. "Not like you."

"I don't care who you had sex with, how many times or who he was. What I do care is that I am the best you've ever had. I'm going to aim to make sure that's the case."

He reached across the table, grabbing hold of her hand. "I'm ready for dessert," he said.

"Me too," she said, pushing her plate back and moving to her feet. "Upstairs?"

He nodded once, the slow burn in his dark eyes searing through her. "Upstairs."

Seven

"Well, it looks like everything is coming together for Dad's Christmas party," Sierra said brightly, looking down at the car seat next to her that contained a sleeping newborn. "Gage will be there, kind of a triumphant return, coming-out kind of thing."

Maddy's older brother shifted in his seat, his arms crossed over his broad chest. "You make me sound like a debutante having a coming-out ball."

"That would be a surprise," his girlfriend, Rebecca Bear, said, putting her hand over his.

"I didn't mean it that way," Sierra said, smiling, her slightly rounder post-childbirth cheeks making her look even younger than she usually did.

Maddy was having a difficult time concentrating. She had met her siblings early at The Grind, the most popular coffee shop in Copper Ridge, so that they could all get on the same page about the big West family soiree that would be thrown on Christmas Eve.

Maddy was ambivalent about it. Mostly she wanted to crawl back under the covers with Sam and burrow until winter passed. But they had agreed that it would go on only until Christmas. Which meant that not only was she dreading the party, it also marked the end of their blissful affair.

By the time Sam had left last night, it had been the next morning, just very early, the sun still inky black as he'd walked out of her house and to his truck.

She had wanted him to stay the entire night, and that was dangerous. She didn't need all that. Didn't need to be held by him, didn't need to wake up in his arms.

"Madison." The sound of her full name jerked her out of her fantasy. She looked up, to see that Colton had been addressing her.

"What?" she asked. "I zoned out for a minute. I haven't had all the caffeine I need yet." Mostly because she had barely slept. She had expected to go out like a light after Sam had left her, but that had not been the case. She had just sort of lay there feeling a little bit achy and lonely and wishing that she didn't.

"Just wondering how you were feeling about Jack coming. You know, now that the whole town knows that he's our half brother, it really is for the best if he comes. I've already talked to Dad about it, and he agrees."

"Great," she said, "and what about Mom?"

"I expect she'll go along with it. She always does. Anyway, Jack is a thirty-five-year-old sin. There's not much use holding it against him now."

"There never was," Maddy said, staring fixedly at her disposable coffee cup, allowing the warm liquid inside to heat her fingertips. She felt like a hypocrite saying that. Mostly because there was something about Jack that was difficult for her.

Well, she knew what it was. The fact that he was evidence of an affair her father had had. The fact that her father was the sort of man who cheated on his wife.

That her father was the sort of man more able to identify with the man who had broken Maddy's heart than he was able to identify with Maddy herself.

But Jack had nothing to do with that. Not really. She knew that logically. He was a good man, married to a great woman, with an adorable baby she really *did* want in her life. It was just that sometimes it needled at her. Got under her skin.

"True enough," Colton said. If he noticed her unease, he certainly didn't betray that he did.

The idea of trying to survive through another West family party just about made her jump up from the coffee shop, run down Main Street and scamper under a rock. She just didn't know if she could do it. Stand there in a pretty dress trying to pretend that she was something the entire town knew she wasn't. Trying to pretend that she was anything other than a disappointment. That her whole family was anything other than tarnished.

Sam didn't feel that way. Not about her. Suddenly, she thought about standing there with him. Sam in a tux, warm and solid next to her...

She blinked, cutting off that line of thinking. There was no reason to be having those fantasies. What she and Sam had was not that. Whatever it was, it wasn't that.

"Then it's settled," Maddy said, a little bit too brightly. "Jack and his family will come to the party."

That sentence made another strange, hollow sensation echo through her. Jack would be there with his family. Sierra and Ace would be there together with their baby. Colton would be there with his wife, Lydia, and while they hadn't made it official yet, Gage and Rebecca were rarely anywhere without each other, and it was plain to anyone who had eyes that Rebecca had changed Gage in a profound way. That she was his support and he was hers.

It was just another way in which Maddy stood alone.

Wow, what a whiny, tragic thought. It wasn't like she wanted her siblings to have nothing. It wasn't like she wanted them to spend their lives alone. Of course she wanted them to have significant others. Maybe she would get around to having one too, eventually.

But it wouldn't be Sam. So she needed to stop

having fantasies about him in that role. Naked fantasies. That was all she was allowed.

"Great," Sierra said, lifting up her coffee cup. "I'm going to go order a coffee for Ace and head back home. He's probably just now getting up. He worked closing at the bar last night and then got up to feed the baby. I owe him caffeine and my eternal devotion. But he will want me to lead with the caffeine." She waved and picked up the bucket seat, heading toward the counter.

"I have to go too," Colton said, leaning forward and kissing Maddy on the cheek. "See you later."

Gage nodded slowly, his dark gaze on Rebecca. She nodded, almost imperceptibly, and stood up. "I'm going to grab a refill," she said, making her way to the counter.

As soon as she was out of earshot, Gage turned his focus to her, and Maddy knew that the refill was only a decoy.

"Are you okay?"

This question, coming from the brother she knew the least, the brother who had been out of her life for seventeen years before coming back into town almost two months ago, was strange. And yet in some ways it wasn't. She had felt, from the moment he had returned, that there was something similar in the two of them.

Something broken and strong that maybe the rest of them couldn't understand.

Since then, she had learned more about the circumstances behind his leaving. The accident that he had been involved in that had left Rebecca Bear scarred as a child. Much to Maddy's surprise, they now seemed to be in love.

Which, while she was happy for him, was also a little annoying. Rebecca was the woman he had damaged—however accidentally—and she could love him, while Maddy seemed to be some kind of remote island no one wanted to connect with.

If she took the Gage approach, she could throw hot coffee on the nearest handsome guy, wait a decade and a half and see if his feelings changed for her over time. However, she imagined that was somewhat unrealistic.

"I'm fine," she said brightly. "Always fine."

"Right. Except I'm used to you sounding dry with notes of sarcasm and today you've been overly peppy and sparkly like a Christmas angel, and I think we both know that isn't real."

"Well, the alternative is me complaining about how this time of year gets me a little bit down, and given the general mood around the table, that didn't seem to be the best idea."

"Right. Why don't you like this time of year?"

"I don't know, Gage. Think back to all the years you spent in solitude on the road. Then tell me how you felt about Christmas."

"At best, it didn't seem to matter much. At worst, it reminded me of when I was happy. When I was home with all of you. And when home felt like a happy place. That was the hardest part, Maddy. Being away and longing for a home I couldn't go back to. Because it didn't exist. Not really. After everything I found out about Dad, I knew it wouldn't ever feel the same."

Her throat tightened, emotion swamping her. She had always known that Gage was the one who would understand her. She had been right. Because no one had ever said quite so perfectly exactly what she felt inside, what she had felt ever since news of her dalliance with her dressage trainer had made its way back to Nathan West's ears.

"It's so strange that you put it that way," she said, "because that is exactly how it feels. I live at home. I never left. And I…I ache for something I can never have again. Even if it's just to see my parents in the way that I used to."

"You saw how it was with all of us sitting here," Gage said. "It's something that I never thought I would have. The fact that you've all been willing to forgive me, to let me back into your lives after I was gone for so long, changes the shape of things. We are the ones that can make it different. We can fix what happened with Jack—or move forward into fixing it. There's no reason you and I can't be fixed too, Maddy."

She nodded, her throat so tight she couldn't speak. She stood, holding her coffee cup against her chest. "I am looking forward to seeing you at the Christmas party." Then she forced a smile and walked out of The Grind.

She took a deep breath of the freezing air, hoping that it might wash some of the stale feelings of sadness and grief right out of her body. Then she looked down Main Street, at all of the Christmas lights gilding the edges of the brick buildings like glimmering precious metal.

Christmas wreaths hung from every surface that would take them, velvet bows a crimson beacon against the intense green.

Copper Ridge at Christmas was beautiful, but walking around, she still felt a bit like a stranger, separate and somehow not a part of it all. Everyone here was so good. People like her and Gage had to leave when they got too bad. Except she hadn't left. She just hovered around the edges like a ghost, making inappropriate and sarcastic comments on demand so that no one would ever look at her too closely and see just what a mess she was.

She lowered her head, the wind whipping through her hair, over her cheeks, as she made her way down the street—the opposite direction of her car. She wasn't really sure what she was doing, only that she couldn't face heading back to the ranch right now. Not when she felt nostalgic for something that didn't exist anymore. When she felt raw from the conversation with Gage.

She kept going down Main, pausing at the front door of the Mercantile when she saw a display of

Christmas candy sitting in the window. It made her smile to see it there, a sugary reminder of some old memory that wasn't tainted by reality.

She closed her eyes tight, and she remembered what it was. Walking down the street with her father, who was always treated like he was a king then. She had been small, and it had been before Gage had left. Before she had ever disappointed anyone.

It was Christmastime, and carolers were milling around, and she had looked up and seen sugarplums and candy canes, little peppermint chocolates and other sweets in the window. He had taken her inside and allowed her to choose whatever she wanted.

A simple memory. A reminder of a time when things hadn't been quite so hard, or quite so real, between herself and Nathan West.

She found herself heading inside, in spite of the fact that the entire point of this walk had been to avoid memories. But then, she really wanted to avoid the memories that were at the ranch. This was different.

She opened the door, taking a deep breath of gingerbread and cloves upon entry. The narrow little store with exposed brick walls was packed with goodies. Cakes, cheeses and breads, imported and made locally.

Lane Jensen, the owner of the Mercantile, was standing toward the back of the store talking to somebody. Maddy didn't see another person right away, and then, when the broad figure came into view, her heart slammed against her breastbone.

When she realized it was Sam, she had to ask herself if she had been drawn down this way because of a sense of nostalgia or because something in her head sensed that he was around. That was silly. Of course she didn't *sense* his presence.

Though, given pheromones and all of that, maybe it wasn't too ridiculous. It certainly wasn't some kind of emotional crap. Not her heart recognizing where his was beating or some such nonsense.

For a split second she considered running the other direction. Before he saw her, before it got weird. But she hesitated, just for the space of a breath, and that was long enough for Sam to look past Lane, his eyes locking with hers.

She stood, frozen to the spot. "Hi," she said, knowing that she sounded awkward, knowing that she looked awkward.

She was unaccustomed to that. At least, these days. She had grown a tough outer shell, trained herself to never feel ashamed, to never feel embarrassed—not in a way that people would be able to see.

Because after her little scandal, she had always imagined that it was the only thing people thought about when they looked at her. Walking around, feeling like that, feeling like you had a scarlet *A* burned into your skin, it forced you to figure out a way to exist.

In her case it had meant cultivating a kind of brash persona. So, being caught like this, looking like a deer in the headlights—which was what she imagined she looked like right now, wide-eyed and trembling—it all felt a bit disorienting.

"Maddy," Sam said, "I wasn't expecting to see you here."

"That's because we didn't make any plans to meet here," she said. "I promise I didn't follow you." She looked over at Lane, who was studying them with great interest. "Not that I would. Because there's no reason for me to do that. Because you're the farrier for my horses. And that's it." She felt distinctly detached and light-headed, as though she might drift away on a cloud of embarrassment at a moment's notice.

"Right," he said. "Thank you, Lane," he said, turning his attention back to the other woman. "I can bring the installation down tomorrow." He tipped his hat, then moved away from Lane, making his way toward her.

"Hi, Lane," she said. Sam grabbed hold of her elbow and began to propel her out of the store. "Bye, Lane."

As soon as they were back out on the street, she rounded on him. "What was that? I thought we were trying to be discreet."

"Lane Jensen isn't a gossip. Anyway, you standing there turning the color of a beet wasn't exactly subtle."

"I am not a beet," she protested, stamping.

"A tiny tomato."

"Stop comparing me to vegetables."

"A tomato isn't a vegetable."

She let out a growl and began to walk away from him, heading back up Main Street and toward her car. "Wait," he said, his voice possessing some kind of unknowable power to actually make her obey.

She stopped, rooted to the cement. "What?"

"We live in the same town. We're going to have to figure out how to interact with each other."

"Or," she said, "we continue on with this very special brand of awkwardness."

"Would it be the worst thing in the world if people knew?"

"You know my past, and you can ask me that?" She looked around the street, trying to see if anybody was watching their little play. "I'm not going to talk to you about this on the town stage."

He closed the distance between them. "Fine. We don't have to have the discussion. And it doesn't matter to me either way. But you really think you should spend the rest of your life punishing yourself for a mistake that happened when you were seventeen? He took advantage of you—it isn't your fault. And apart from any of that, you don't deserve to be labeled by a bunch of people that don't even know you."

That wasn't even it. And as she stood there, staring him down, she realized that fully. It had nothing to do with what the town thought. Nothing to do with whether or not the town thought she was a scarlet woman, or if people still thought about her indiscretion, or if people blamed her or David. None of that mattered.

She realized that in a flash of blinding brilliance that shone brighter than the Christmas lights all around her. And that realization made her knees buckle, because it made her remember the conversation that had happened in her father's office. The conversation that had occurred right after one of David's students had discovered the affair between the two of them and begun spreading rumors.

Rumors that were true, regrettably.

Rumors that had made their way all the way back to Nathan West's home office.

"I can't talk about this right now," she said, brushing past him and striding down the sidewalk.

"You don't have to talk about it with me, not ever. But what's going to happen when this is over? You're going to go another ten years between lovers? Just break down and hold your breath and do it again when you can't take the celibacy anymore?"

"Stop it," she said, walking faster.

"Like I said, it doesn't matter to me…"

She whirled around. "You keep saying it doesn't matter to you, and then you keep pushing the issue. So I would say that it does matter to you. Whatever complex you have about not being good enough, this is digging at that. But it isn't my problem. Because it isn't about you. Nobody would care if they knew that we were sleeping together. I mean, they would talk about it, but they wouldn't care. But it makes it something more. And I just… I can't have more. Not more than this."

He shifted uncomfortably. "Well, neither can I. That was hardly an invitation for something deeper."

"Good. Because I don't have anything deeper to give."

The very idea made her feel like she was going into a free fall. The idea of trusting somebody again…

The betrayals she had dealt with back when she was seventeen had made it so that trusting another human being was almost unfathomable. When she had told Sam that the sex was the least of it, she had been telling the truth.

It had very little to do with her body, and everything to do with the battering her soul had taken.

"Neither do I."

"Then why are you… Why are you pushing me like this?"

He looked stunned by the question, his face frozen. "I just… I don't want to leave you broken."

Something inside her softened, cracked a little bit. "I'm not sure that you have a choice. It kind of is what it is, you know?"

"Maybe it doesn't have to be."

"Did you think you were going to fix me, Sam?"

"No," he said, his voice rough.

But she knew he was lying. "Don't put that on yourself. Two broken people can't fix each other."

She was certain in that moment that he was broken too, even though she wasn't quite sure how.

"We only have twelve days. Any kind of fixing was a bit ambitious anyway," he said.

"Eleven days," she reminded him. "I'll see you tonight?"

"Yeah. See you then."

And then she turned and walked away from Sam McCormack for all the town to see, as if he were just a casual acquaintance and nothing more. And she tried to ignore the ache in the center of her chest that didn't seem to go away, even after she got in the car and drove home.

Eight

Seven days after beginning the affair with Maddy, she called and asked him if he could come down and check the shoes on one of the horses. It was the middle of the afternoon, so if it was her version of a booty call, he thought it was kind of an odd time. And since their entire relationship was a series of those, he didn't exactly see why she wouldn't be up front about it.

But when he showed up, she was waiting for him outside the stall.

"What are you up to?"

She lifted her shoulder. "I just wanted you to come and check on the horse."

"Something you couldn't check yourself?"

She looked slightly rueful. "Okay, maybe I could

have checked it myself. But she really is walking a little bit funny, and I'm wondering if something is off."

She opened the stall door, clipped a lead rope to the horse's harness and brought her out into the main part of the barn.

He looked at her, then pushed up the sleeves on his thermal shirt and knelt down in front of the large animal, drawing his hand slowly down her leg and lifting it gently. Then he did the same to the next before moving to her hindquarters and repeating the motion again.

He stole a glance up at Maddy, who was staring at him with rapt attention.

"What?"

"I like watching you work," she said. "I've always liked watching you work. That's why I used to come down here and give orders. Okay, honestly? I wanted to give myself permission to watch you and enjoy it." She swallowed hard. "You're right. I've been punishing myself. So, I thought I might indulge myself."

"I'm going to have to charge your dad for this visit," he said.

"He won't notice," she said. "Trust me."

"I don't believe that. Your father is a pretty well-known businessman." He straightened, petting the horse on its haunches. "Everything looks fine."

Maddy looked sheepish. "Great."

"Why don't you think your dad would notice?"

"A lot of stuff has come out over the past few

months. You know he had a stroke three months
ago or so, and while he's recovered pretty well since
then, it changed things. I mean, it didn't change *him*.
It's not like he miraculously became some soft, easy
man. Though, I think he's maybe a little bit more in
touch with his mortality. Not happily, mind you, I
think he always saw himself as something of a god."

"Well," Sam said, "what man doesn't?" At least,
until he was set firmly back down to earth and reminded of just how badly he could mess things up.
How badly things could hurt.

"Yet another difference between men and women,"
Maddy said drily. "But after he had his stroke, the
control of the finances went to my brother Gage.
That was why he came back to town initially. He discovered that there was a lot of debt. I mean, I know
you've heard about how many properties we've had
to sell downtown."

Sam stuffed his hands in his pockets, lifting his
shoulders. "Not really. But then, I don't exactly keep
up on that kind of stuff. That's Chase's arena. Busi-
nesses and the real estate market. That's not me. I
just screw around with metal."

"You downplay what you do," she returned. "From
the art to the physical labor. I've watched you do it.
I don't know why you do it, only that you do. You're
always acting like your brother is smarter than you,
but he can't do what you do either."

"Art was never particularly useful as far as my
father was concerned," Sam said. "I imagine he

would be pretty damned upset to see that it's the art that keeps the ranch afloat so nicely. He would have wanted us to do it the way our ancestors did. Making leatherwork and pounding nails. Of course, it was always hard for him to understand that mass production was inevitably going to win out against more expensive handmade things. Unless we targeted our products and people who could afford what we did. Which is what we did. What we've been successful with far beyond what we even imagined."

"Dads," she said, her voice soft. "They do get in your head, don't they?"

"I mean, my father didn't have gambling debts and a secret child, but he was kind of a difficult bastard. I still wish he wasn't dead." He laughed. "It would kind of be nice to have him wandering around the place shaking his head disapprovingly as I loaded up that art installation to take down to the Mercantile."

"I don't know, having your dad hanging around disapproving is kind of overrated." Suddenly, her face contorted with horror. "I'm sorry—I had no business saying something like that. It isn't fair. I shouldn't make light of your loss."

"It was a long time ago. And anyway, I do it all the time. I think it's the way the emotionally crippled deal with things." Anger. Laughter. It was all better than hurt.

"Yeah," she said, laughing uneasily. "That sounds about right."

"What exactly does your dad disapprove of, Madison?" he asked, reverting back to her full name. He kind of liked it, because nobody else called her that. And she had gone from looking like she wanted to claw his eyes out when he used it to responding. There was something that felt deep about that. Connected. He shouldn't care. If anything, it should entice him not to do it. But it didn't.

"Isn't it obvious?"

"No," he returned. "I've done a lot of work on this ranch over the years. You're always busy. You have students scheduled all day every day—except today, apparently—and it is a major part of both the reputation and the income of this facility. You've poured everything you have into reinforcing his legacy while letting your own take a backseat."

"Well, when you put it like that," she said, the smile on her lips obviously forced, "I am kind of amazing."

"What exactly does he disapprove of?"

"What do you think?"

"Does it all come back to that? Something you did when you were seventeen?" The hypocrisy of the outrage in his tone wasn't lost on him.

"I'm not sure," she said, the words biting. "I'm really not." She grabbed hold of the horse's lead rope, taking her back into the stall before clipping the rope and coming back out, shutting the door firmly.

"What do you mean by that?"

She growled, making her way out of the barn and walking down the paved path that led toward one of the covered arenas. "I don't know. Feel free to choose your own adventure with that one."

"Come on, Maddy," he said, closing the distance between them and lowering his voice. "I've tasted parts of you that most other people have never seen. A little bit of honesty isn't going to hurt you."

She whipped around, her eyes bright. "Maybe it isn't him. Maybe it's me. Maybe I'm the one that can't look at him the same way."

Maddy felt rage simmering over her skin like heat waves. She had not intended to have this conversation—not with Sam, not with anyone.

But now she had started, she didn't know if she could stop. "The night that he found out about my affair with David was the night I found out about Jack."

"So, it isn't a recent revelation to all of you?"

"No," she said. "Colton and Sierra didn't know. I'm sure of that. But I found out that Gage did. I didn't know who it was, I should clarify. I just found out that he had another child." She looked away from Sam, trying to ignore the burning sensation in her stomach. Like there was molten lava rolling around in there. She associated that feeling with being called into her father's home office.

It had always given her anxiety, even before everything had happened with David. Even before she had ever seriously disappointed him.

Nathan West was exacting, and Maddy had wanted nothing more than to please him. That desire took up much more of her life than she had ever wanted it to. But then, she knew that was true in some way or another for all of her siblings. It was why Sierra had gone to school for business. Why Colton had taken over the construction company. It was even what had driven Gage to leave.

It was the reason Maddy had poured all of her focus into dressage. Because she had anticipated becoming great. Going to the Olympics. And she knew her father had anticipated that. Then she had ruined all of it.

But not as badly as he had ruined the relationship between the two of them.

"Like I told you, one of David's other students caught us together. Down at the barn where he gave his lessons. We were just kissing, but it was definitely enough. That girl told her father, who in turn went to mine as a courtesy."

Sam laughed, a hard, bitter sound. "A courtesy to who?"

"Not to me," Maddy said. "Or maybe it was. I don't know. It was so awful. The whole situation. I wish there had been a less painful way for it to end. But it had to end, whether it ended that way or some other way, so…so I guess that worked as well as anything."

"Except you had to deal with your father. And then rumors were spread anyway."

She looked away from Sam. "Well, the rumors I kind of blame on David. Because once his wife knew, own father, who should have been on my side simp because I was born his. I loved them both. And th both let me down." She blinked, a mist rolling ov her insides, matching the setting all around then "How do you ever trust anyone after that? If it ha only been David. I think I would have been over a long time ago."

Sam was looking at her, regarding her with dark intense eyes. He looked like he was about to say something, his chest shifting as he took in a breath that seemed to contain purpose. But then he said nothing. He simply closed the distance between them, tugging her into his arms, holding her against his chest, his large, warm hand moving between her shoulder blades in a soothing rhythm.

She hadn't rested on anyone in longer than she could remember. Hadn't been held like this in years. Her mother was too brittle to lean on. She would break beneath the weight of somebody else's sorrow. Her father had never offered a word of comfort to anyone. And she had gotten in the habit of pretending she was tough so that Colton and Sierra wouldn't worry about her. So that they wouldn't look too deeply at how damaged she was still from the events of the past.

So she put all her weight on him and total peace washed over her. She shouldn't indulge in this. She shouldn't allow herself this. It was dangerous. But she couldn't stop. And she didn't want to.

She squeezed her eyes shut, a few more tears fall-

there was really no reason for the whole world not to know. And I think it suited him to paint me in an unflattering light. He took a gamble. A gamble that the man in the situation would come out of it all just fine. It was not a bad gamble, it turned out."

"I guess not."

"Full house. Douche bag takes the pot."

She was avoiding the point of this conversation. Avoiding the truth of it. She didn't even know why she should tell him. She didn't know why anything. Except that she had never confided any of this to anyone before. She was close to her sister, and Sierra had shared almost everything about her relationship with Ace with Maddy, and here Maddy was keeping more secrets from her.

She had kept David from her. She had kept Sam from her too. And she had kept this all to herself, as well.

She knew why. In a blinding flash she knew why. She couldn't stand being rejected, not again. She had been rejected by her first love; she had been rejected by an entire community. She had been rejected by her father with a few cold dismissive words in his beautifully appointed office in her childhood home.

But maybe, just maybe, that was why she should confide in Sam. Because at the end of their affair it wouldn't matter. Because then they would go back to sniping at each other or not talking to each other at all.

Because he hadn't rejected her yet.

"When he called me into his office, I knew I was in trouble," she said, rubbing her hand over her forehead. "He never did that for good things. Ever. If there was something good to discuss, we would talk about it around the dinner table. Only bad things were ever talked about in his office with the door firmly closed. He talked to Gage like that. Right before he left town. So, I always knew it had to be bad."

She cleared her throat, looking out across the arena, through the gap in the trees and at the distant view of the misty waves beyond. It was so very gray, the clouds hanging low in the sky, touching the top of the angry, steel-colored sea.

"Anyway, I *knew*. As soon as I walked in, I knew. He looked grim. Like I've never seen him before. And he asked me what was going on with myself and David Smithson. Well, I knew there was no point in denying it. So I told him. He didn't yell. I wish he had. He said... He said the worst thing you could ever do was get caught. That a man like David spent years building up his reputation, not to have it undone by the temptation of some young girl." She blinked furiously. "He said that if a woman was going to present more temptation than a man could handle, the least she could do was keep it discreet."

"How could he say that to you? To his daughter? Look, my dad was a difficult son of a bitch, but if he'd had a daughter and some man had hurt her, he'd have ridden out on his meanest stallion with a pair of pliers to dole out the world's least sterile castration."

Maddy choked out a laugh that was mixed with a sob. "That's what I thought. It really was. I thought... I thought he would be angry, but one of the things that scared me most, at least initially, was the idea that he would take it out on David. And I still loved David then. But no. He was angry at me."

"I don't understand how that's possible."

"That was when he told me," she choked out. "Told me that he had mistresses, that it was just something men did, but that the world didn't run if the mistress didn't know her place, and if I was intent on lowering myself to be that sort of woman when I could have easily been a wife, that was none of his business. He told me a woman had had his child and never betrayed him." Her throat tightened, almost painfully, a tear sliding down her cheek. "Even he saw me as the villain. If my own father couldn't stand up for me, if even he thought it was my fault somehow, how was I ever supposed to stand up for myself when other people accused me of being a whore?"

"Maddy..."

"That's why," she said, the words thin, barely making their way through her constricted throat. "That's why it hurts so much. And that's why I'm not over it. There were two men involved in that who said they loved me. There was David, the man I had given my heart to, the man I had given my body to, who had lied to me from the very beginning, who threw me under the bus the moment he got the opportunity. And then there was my own father. My

ing down her cheeks, soaking into his shirt. If anybody knew that Madison West had wept all over a man in the broad light of day, they wouldn't believe it. But she didn't care. This wasn't about anyone else. It was just about her. About purging her soul of some of the poison that had taken up residence there ten years ago and never quite left.

About dealing with some of the heavy longing that existed inside her for a time and a place she could never return to. For a Christmas when she had walked down Main Street with her father and seen him as a hero.

But of course, when she was through crying, she felt exposed. Horribly. Hideously, and she knew this was why she didn't make a habit out of confiding in people. Because now Sam McCormack knew too much about her. Knew more about her than maybe anybody else on earth. At least, he knew about parts of her that no one else did.

The tenderness. The insecurity. The parts that were on the verge of cracking open, crumbling the foundation of her and leaving nothing more than a dusty pile of Maddy behind.

She took a deep breath, hoping that the pressure would squeeze some of those shattering pieces of herself back together with the sheer force of it. Too bad it just made her aware of more places down deep that were compromised.

Still, she wiggled out of his grasp, needing a moment to get ahold of herself. Needing very much to not get caught being held by a strange man down at the arena by any of the staff or anyone in her family.

"Thank you," she said, her voice shaking. "I just... I didn't know how much I needed that."

"I didn't do anything."

"You listened. You didn't try to give me advice or tell me I was wrong. That's actually doing a lot. A lot more than most people are willing to do."

"So, do you want me to come back here tonight?"

"Actually," she said, grabbing hold of her hands, twisting them, trying to deal with the nervous energy that was rioting through her, "I was thinking maybe I could come out a little bit early. And I could see where you work."

She didn't know why she was doing this. She didn't know where she imagined it could possibly end or how it would be helpful to her in any way. To add more pieces of him to her heart, to her mind.

That's what it felt like she was trying to do. Like collecting shells on the seashore. Picking up all the shimmering pieces of Sam she possibly could and sticking them in her little pail, hoarding them. Making a collection.

For what? Maybe for when it was over.

Maybe that wasn't so bad.

She had pieces of David, whether she wanted them or not. And she'd entertained the idea that maybe she could sleep with someone and not do that. Not carry them forward with her.

But the reality of it was that she wasn't going to

walk away from this affair and never think of Sam again. He was never going to be the farrier again. He would always be Sam. Why not leave herself with beautiful memories instead of terrible ones? Maybe this was what she needed to do.

"You want to see the forge?" he asked.

"Sure. That would be interesting. But also your studio. I'm curious about your art, and I realize that I don't really know anything about it. Seeing you in the Mercantile the other day talking to Lane…" She didn't know how to phrase what she was thinking without sounding a little bit crazy. Without sounding overly attached. So she just let the sentence trail off.

But she was curious. She was curious about him. About who he was when he wasn't here. About who he was as a whole person, without the blinders around him that she had put there. She had very purposefully gone out of her way to know nothing about him. And so he had always been Sam McCormack, grumpy guy who worked at her family ranch on occasion and who she often bantered with in the sharpest of senses.

But there was more to him. So much more. This man who had held her, this man who had listened, this man who seemed to know everyone in town and have decent relationships with them. Who created beautiful things that started in his mind and were then formed with his hands. She wanted to know him.

Yeah, she wouldn't be telling him any of that.

"Were you jealous? Because there is nothing between myself and Lane Jensen. First of all, anyone who wants anything to do with her has to go through Finn Donnelly, and I have no desire to step in the middle of *that* weird dynamic and his older-brother complex."

It struck her then that jealousy hadn't even been a component to what she had felt the other day. How strange. Considering everything she had been through with men, it seemed like maybe trust should be the issue here. But it wasn't. It never had been.

It had just been this moment of catching sight of him at a different angle. Like a different side to a prism that cast a different color on the wall and made her want to investigate further. To see how one person could contain so many different things.

A person who was so desperate to hide anything beyond that single dimension he seemed comfortable with.

Another thing she would definitely not say to him. She couldn't imagine the twenty shades of rainbow horror that would cross Sam's face if she compared him to a prism out loud.

"I was not," she said. "But it made me aware of the fact that you're kind of a big deal. And I haven't fully appreciated that."

"Of course you haven't," he said, his tone dry. "It interferes with your stable-boy fantasy."

She made a scoffing sound. "I do not have a stable-boy fantasy."

"Yes, you do. You like slumming it."

Those words called up heated memories out of the depths of her mind. Him whispering things in her ear. His rough hands skimming over her skin. She bit her lip. "I like nothing of the kind, Sam Mc-Cormack. Not with you, not with any man. Are you going to show me your pretty art or not?"

"Not if you call it pretty."

"You'll have to take your chances. I'm not putting a cap on my vocabulary for your comfort. Anyway, if you haven't noticed, unnerving people with what I may or may not say next is kind of my thing."

"I've noticed."

"You do it too," she said.

His lips tipped upward into a small smile. "Do I?"

She rolled her eyes. "Oh, don't pretend you don't know. You're way too smart for that. And you act like the word *smart* is possibly the world's most vile swear when it's applied to you. But you are. You can throw around accusations of slumming it all you want, but if we didn't connect mentally, and if I didn't respect you in some way, this wouldn't work."

"Our brains have nothing to do with this."

She lifted a finger. "A woman's largest sexual organ is her brain."

He chuckled, wrapping his arm around her waist and drawing her close. "Sure, Maddy. But we both know what the most important one is." He leaned in, whispering dirty things in her ear, and she laughed, pushing against his chest. "Okay," he said, finally. "I will let you come see my studio."

She fought against the trickle of warmth that ran through her, that rested deep in her stomach and spread out from there, making her feel a kind of languid satisfaction that she had no business feeling over something like this. "Then I guess I'll see you for the art show."

Nine

Sam had no idea what in hell had possessed him to let Maddy come out to his property tonight. Chase and Anna were not going to let this go ignored. In fact, Anna was already starting to make comments about the fact that he hadn't been around for dinner recently. Which was why he was there tonight, eating as quickly as possible so he could get back out to his place on the property before Maddy arrived. He had given her directions to go on the road that would allow her to bypass the main house, which Chase and Anna inhabited.

"Sam." His sister-in-law's voice cut into his thoughts. "I thought you were going to join us for dinner tonight?"

"I'm here," he said.

"Your body is. Your brain isn't. And Chase worked very hard on this meal," Anna said.

Anna was a tractor mechanic, and formerly Chase's best friend in a platonic sense. All of that had come to an end a few months ago when they had realized there was a lot more between them than friendship.

Still, the marriage had not transformed Anna into a domestic goddess. Instead, it had forced Chase to figure out how to share a household with somebody. They were never going to have a traditional relationship, but it seemed to suit Chase just fine.

"It's very good, Chase," Sam said, keeping his tone dry.

"Thanks," Chase said, "I opened the jar of pasta sauce myself."

"Sadly, no one in this house is ever going to win a cooking competition," Anna said.

"You keep *me* from starving," Sam pointed out.

Though, in all honesty, he was a better cook than either of them. Still, it was an excuse to get together with his brother. And sometimes it felt like he needed excuses. So that he didn't have to think deeply about a feeling that was more driving than hunger pangs.

"Not recently," Chase remarked. "You haven't been around."

Sam let out a heavy sigh. "Yes, sometimes a man assumes that newlyweds want time alone without their crabby brother around."

"We always want you around," Anna said. Then she screwed up her face. "Okay, we don't *always* want you around. But for dinner, when we invite you, it's fine."

"Just no unexpected visits to the house," Chase said. "In the evening. Or anytime. And maybe also don't walk into Anna's shop without knocking after hours."

Sam grimaced. "I get the point. Anyway, I've just been busy. And I'm about to be busy again." He stood up, anticipation shooting through him. He had gone a long time without sex, and now sex with Maddy was about all he could think about. Five years of celibacy would do that to a man.

Made a man do stupid things, like invite the woman he was currently sleeping with to come to his place and to come see his art. Whatever the hell she thought that would entail. He was inclined to figure it out. Just so she would feel happy, so he could see her smile again.

So she would be in the mood to put out. And nothing more. Certainly no emotional reasoning behind that.

He couldn't do that. Not ever again.

"Okay," Anna said, "you're always cagey, Sam, I'll give you that. But you have to give me a hint about what's going on."

"No," Sam said, turning to go. "I really don't."

"Sculpture? A woman?"

Well, sadly, Anna was mostly on point with both. "Not your business."

"That's hilarious," Chase said, "coming from the man who meddled in our relationship."

"You jackasses needed meddling," Sam said. "You were going to let her go." Of the two of them, Chase was undoubtedly the better man. And Anna was one of the best, man or woman. When Sam had realized his brother was about to let Anna get away because of baggage from his past, Sam had had no choice but to play the older-brother card and give advice that he himself would never have taken.

But it was different for Chase. Sam wanted it to be different for Chase. He didn't want his younger brother living the same stripped-down existence he did.

"Well, maybe you need meddling too, jackass," Anna said.

Sam ignored his sister-in-law and continued on out of the house, taking the steps on the porch two at a time, the frosted ground crunching beneath his boots as he walked across the field, taking the short route between the two houses.

He shoved his hands in his pockets, looking up, watching his breath float up into the dense sky, joining the mist there. It was already getting dark, the twilight hanging low around him, a deep blue ink spill that bled down over everything.

It reminded him of grief. A darkness that descended without warning, covering everything around it, changing it. Taking things that were familiar and twisting them into foreign objects and strangers.

That thought nibbled at the back of his mind.

He couldn't let it go. It just hovered there as he made his way back to his place, trying to push its way to the front of his mind and form the obvious conclusion.

He resisted it. The way that he always did. Anytime he got inspiration that seemed related to these kinds of feelings. And then he would go out to his shop and start working on another Texas longhorn sculpture. Because that didn't mean anything and people would want to buy it.

Just as he approached his house, so did Maddy's car. She parked right next to his truck, and a strange feeling of domesticity overtook him. Two cars in the driveway. His and hers.

He pushed that aside too.

He watched her open the car door, her blond hair even paler in the advancing moonlight. She was wearing a hat, the shimmering curls spilling out from underneath it. She also had on a scarf and gloves. And there was something about her, looking soft and bundled up, and very much not like prickly, brittle Maddy, that made him want to pull her back into his arms like he had done earlier that day and hold her up against his chest.

Hold her until she quit shaking. Or until she started shaking for a different reason entirely.

"You made it," he said.

"You say that like you had some doubt that I would."

"Well, at the very least I thought you might change your mind."

"No such luck for you. I'm curious. And once my curiosity is piqued, I will have it satisfied."

"You're like a particularly meddlesome cat," he said.

"You're going to have to make up your mind, Sam," Maddy said, smiling broadly.

"About what?"

"Am I vegetable or mammal? You have now compared me to both."

"A tomato is a fruit."

"Whatever," she said, waving a gloved hand.

"Do you want to come out and see the sculptures or do you want to stand here arguing about whether or not you're animal, vegetable or mineral?"

Her smile only broadened. "Sculptures, please."

"Well, follow me. And it's a good thing you bundled up."

"This is how much I had to bundle to get in the car and drive over here. My heater is *not* broken. I didn't know that I was going to be wandering around out in the dark, in the cold."

He snorted. "You run cold?"

"I do."

"I hadn't noticed."

She lifted a shoulder, taking two steps to his every one, doing her best to keep up with him as he led them both across the expanse of frozen field. "Well, I'm usually very hot when you're around. Anyway, the combination of you and blankets is very warming."

"What happens when I leave?"

"I get cold," she returned.

Something about those words felt like a knife in the center of his chest. Damned if he knew why. At least, damned if he wanted to know why.

What he wanted was to figure out how to make it go away.

They continued on the rest of the walk in silence, and he increased his pace when the shop came into view. "Over here is where Chase and I work," he said, gesturing to the first building. "Anna's is on a different section of the property, one closer to the road so that it's easier for her customers to get in there, since they usually have heavy equipment being towed by heavier equipment. And this one is mine." He pointed to another outbuilding, one that had once been a separate machine shed.

"We remodeled it this past year. Expanded and made room for the new equipment. I have a feeling my dad would piss himself if he knew what this was being used for now," he continued, not quite able to keep the thought in his mind.

Maddy came up beside him, looping her arm through his. "Maybe. But I want to see it. And I promise you I won't...do *that*."

"Appreciated," he said, allowing her to keep hold of him while they walked inside.

He realized then that nobody other than Chase

and Anna had ever been in here. And he had never grandly showed it to either of them. They just popped in on occasion to let him know that lunch or dinner was ready or to ask if he was ever going to resurface.

He had never invited anyone here. Though, he supposed that Maddy had invited herself here. Either way, this was strange. It was exposing in a way he hadn't anticipated it being. Mostly because that required he admit that there was something of himself in his work. And he resisted that. Resisted it hard.

It had always been an uncomfortable fit for him. That he had this ability, this compulsion to create things, that could come only from inside him. Which was a little bit like opening up his chest and showing bits of it to the world. Which was the last thing on earth he ever wanted to do. He didn't like sharing himself with other people. Not at all.

Maddy turned a slow circle, her soft, pink mouth falling open. "Wow," she said. "Is this all of them?"

"No," he said, following her line of sight, looking at the various iron sculptures all around them. Most of them were to scale with whatever they were representing. Giant two-ton metal cows and horses, one with a cowboy upon its back, took up most of the space in the room.

Pieces that came from what he saw. From a place he loved. But not from inside him.

"What are these?"

"Works in progress, mostly. Almost all of them are close to being done. Which was why I was up at the cabin, remember? I'm trying to figure out what I'm going to do next. But I can always make more things like this. They sell. I can put them in places around town and tourists will always come in and buy them. People pay obscene amounts of money for stuff like this." He let out a long, slow breath. "I'm kind of mystified by it."

"You shouldn't be. It's amazing." She moved around the space, reaching out and brushing her fingertips over the back of one of the cows. "We have to get some for the ranch. They're perfect."

Something shifted in his chest, a question hovering on the tip of his tongue. But he held it back. He had been about to ask her if he should do something different. If he should follow that compulsion that had hit him on the walk back. Those ideas about grief. About loss.

Who the hell wanted to look at something like that? Anyway, he didn't want to show anyone that part of himself. And he sure as hell didn't deserve to profit off any of his losses.

He gritted his teeth. "Great."

"You sound like you think it's great," she said, her tone deeply insincere.

"I wasn't aware my enthusiasm was going to be graded."

She looked around, the shop light making her hair look even deeper gold than it normally did. She reached up, grabbing the knit hat on her head and flinging it onto the ground. He knew what she was doing. He wanted to stop her. Because this was his shop. His studio. It was personal in a way that nothing else was. She could sleep in his bed. She could go to his house, stay there all night, and it would never be the same as her getting naked here.

He was going to stop her.

But then she grabbed the zipper tab on her jacket and shrugged it off before taking hold of the hem of her top, yanking it over her head and sending it the same way as her outerwear.

Then Maddy was standing there, wearing nothing but a flimsy lace bra, the pale curve of her breasts rising and falling with every breath she took.

"Since it's clear how talented your hands are, particularly here…" she said, looking all wide-eyed and innocent. He loved that. The way she could look like this, then spew profanities with the best of them. The way she could make her eyes all dewy, then do something that would make even the most hardened cowboy blush. "I thought I might see if I could take advantage of the inspirational quality of the place."

Immediately, his blood ran hotter, faster, desire roaring in him like a beast. He wanted her. He wanted this. There was nowhere soft to take her, not here. Not in this place full of nails and iron, in this place that was hard and jagged just like his soul, that was more evidence of what he contained than anyone would ever know.

"The rest," he said, his voice as uncompromising

as the sculpture all around them. "Take off the rest, Madison."

Her lashes fluttered as she looked down, undoing the snap on her jeans, then the zipper, maddeningly slowly. And of course, she did her best to look like she had no idea what she was doing to him.

She pushed her jeans down her hips, and all that was left covering her was those few pale scraps of lace. She was so soft. And everything around her was so hard.

It should make him want to protect her. Should make him want to get her out of here. Away from this place. Away from him. But it didn't. He was that much of a bastard.

He didn't take off any of his own clothes, because there was something about the contrast that turned him on even more. Instead, he moved toward her, slowly, not bothering to hide his open appreciation for her curves.

He closed the distance between them, wrapping his hand around the back of her head, sifting his fingers through her hair before tightening his hold on her, tugging gently. She gasped, following his lead, tilting her face upward.

He leaned in, and he could tell that she was expecting a kiss. By the way her lips softened, by the way her eyes fluttered closed. Instead, he angled his head, pressing his lips to that tender skin on her neck. She shivered, the contact clearly an unexpected surprise. But not an unwelcome one.

He kept his fingers buried firmly in her hair, holding her steady as he shifted again, brushing his mouth over the line of her collarbone, following it all the way toward the center of her chest and down to the plush curves of her breasts.

He traced that feathery line there where lace met skin with the tip of his tongue, daring to delve briefly beneath the fabric, relishing the hitch in her breathing when he came close to her sensitized nipples.

He slid his hands up her arms, grabbed hold of the delicate bra straps and tugged them down, moving slowly, ever so slowly, bringing the cups down just beneath her breasts, exposing those dusky nipples to him.

"Beautiful," he said. "Prettier than anything in here."

"I didn't think you wanted the word *pretty* uttered in here," she said, breathless.

"About my work. About you… That's an entirely different situation. You are pretty. These are pretty." He leaned in, brushing his lips lightly over one tightened bud, relishing the sweet sound of pleasure that she made.

"Now who's a tease?" she asked, her voice labored.

"I haven't even started to tease you yet."

He slid his hands around her back, pressing his palms hard between her shoulder blades, lowering his head so that he could draw the center of her breast deep into his mouth. He sucked hard until she whimpered, until she squirmed against him, clearly looking for some kind of relief for the intense arousal that he was building inside her.

He looked up, really looked at her face, a deep, primitive sense of pleasure washing through him. That he was touching such a soft, beautiful woman. That he was allowing himself such an indulgence. That he was doing this to her.

He had forgotten. He had forgotten what it was like to really relish the fact that he possessed the power to make a woman feel good. Because he had reduced his hands to something else entirely. Hands that had failed him, that had failed Elizabeth.

Hands that could form iron into impossible shapes but couldn't be allowed to handle something this fragile.

But here he was with Madison. She was soft, and he wasn't breaking her. She was beautiful, and she was his.

Not yours. Never yours.

He tightened his hold on her, battling the unwelcome thoughts that were trying to crowd in, trying to take over this experience, this moment. When Madison was gone, he would go back to the austere existence he'd been living for the past five years. But right now, he had her, and he wasn't going to let anything damage that. Not now.

Instead of thinking, which was never a good thing, not for him, he continued his exploration of her body. Lowering himself down to his knees in front of her, kissing her just beneath her breasts, and down lower, tracing a line across her soft stomach.

She was everything a woman should be. He was confident of that. Because she was the only woman he could remember. Right now, she was everything.

He moved his hands down her thighs, then back up again, pushing his fingertips beneath the waistband of her panties as he gripped her hips and leaned in, kissing her just beneath her belly button. She shook beneath him, a sweet little trembling that betrayed just how much she wanted him.

She wouldn't, if she knew. If she knew, she wouldn't want him. But she didn't know. And she never had to. There were only five days left. They would never have to talk about it. Ever. They would only ever have this. That was important. Because if they ever tried to have more, there would be nothing. She would run so far the other direction he would never see her again.

Or maybe she wouldn't. Maybe she would stick around. But that was even worse. Because of what he would have to do.

He flexed his fingers, the blunt tips digging into that soft skin at her hips. He growled, moving them around to cup her ass beneath the thin lace fabric on her panties. He squeezed her there too and she moaned, her obvious enjoyment of his hands all over her body sending a surge of pleasure through him.

He shifted, delving between her thighs, sliding his fingers through her slick folds, moving his fingers over her clit before drawing them back, pushing one finger inside her.

She gasped, grabbing his shoulders, pitching forward. He could feel her thigh muscles shaking as he pleasured her slowly, drawing his finger in and out of her body before adding a second. Her nails dug into his skin, clinging to him harder and harder as he continued tormenting her.

He looked up at her and allowed himself to get lost in this. In the feeling of her slick arousal beneath his hands, in the completely overwhelmed, helpless expression on her beautiful face. Her eyes were shut tight, and she was biting her lip, probably to keep herself from screaming. He decided he had a new goal.

He lowered his head, pressing his lips right to the center of her body, her lace panties holding the warmth of his breath as he slowly lapped at her through the thin fabric.

She swore, a short, harsh sound that verged on being a scream. But it wasn't enough. He teased her that way, his fingers deep inside her, his mouth on her, for as long as he could stand it.

Then he took his other hand, swept the panties aside and pushed his fingers in deep while he lapped at her bare skin, dragging his tongue through her folds, over that sensitized bundle of nerves.

And then she screamed.

Her internal muscles pulsed around him, her pleasure ramping his up two impossible degrees.

"I hope like *hell* you brought a condom," he said, his voice ragged, rough.

"I think I did," she said, her tone wavering. "Yes, I did. It's in my purse. Hurry."

"You want me to dig through your purse."

"I can't breathe. I can't move. If I do anything, I'm going to fall down. So I suggest you get the condom so that I don't permanently wound myself attempting to procure it."

"Your tongue seems fine," he said, moving away from her and going to grab the purse that she had discarded along with the rest of her clothes.

"So does yours," she muttered.

And he knew that what she was referring to had nothing to do with talking.

He found the condom easily enough, since it was obviously the last thing she had thrown into her bag. Then he stood, stripping his shirt off and his pants, adding to the pile of clothing that Maddy had already left on the studio floor.

Then he tore open the packet and took care of the protection. He looked around the room, searching for some surface that he could use. That they could use.

There was no way to lay her down, which he kind of regretted. Mostly because he always felt like she deserved a little bit more than the rough stuff that he doled out to her. Except she seemed to like it. So if it was what she wanted, she was about to get the full experience tonight.

He wrapped his arm around her waist, pulling

her up against him, pressing their bodies together, her bare breasts pressing hard against his chest. He was so turned on, his arousal felt like a crowbar between them.

She didn't seem to mind.

He took hold of her chin, tilting her face up so she had to look at him. And then he leaned in, kissing her lightly, gently. It would be the last gentle thing he did all night.

He slid his hands along her body, moving them to grip her hips. Then he turned her so that she was facing away from him. She gasped but followed the momentum as he propelled her forward, toward one of the iron figures—a horse—and placed his hand between her shoulder blades.

"Hold on to the horse, cowgirl," he said, his voice so rough it sounded like a stranger's.

"What?"

He pushed more firmly against her back, bending her forward slightly, and she lifted her hands, placing them over the back of the statue. "Just like that," he said.

Her back arched slightly, and he drew his fingertips down the line of her spine, all the way down to her butt. He squeezed her there, then slipped his hand to her hip.

"Spread your legs," he instructed.

She did, widening her stance, allowing him a good view and all access. He moved his hand back there, just for a second, testing her readiness. Then he positioned his arousal at the entrance to her body. He pushed into her, hard and deep, and she let out a low, slow sound of approval.

He braced himself, putting one hand on her shoulder, his thumb pressed firmly against the back of her neck, the other holding her hip as he began to move inside her.

He lost himself. In her, in the moment. In this soft, beautiful woman, all curves and round shapes in the middle of this hard, angular garden of iron.

The horse was hard in front of her; he was hard behind her. Only Maddy was soft.

Her voice was soft—the little gasps of pleasure that escaped her lips like balm for his soul. Her body was soft, her curves giving against him every time he thrust home.

When she began to rock back against him, her desperation clearly increasing along with his, he moved his hand from her hip to between her thighs. He stroked her in time with his thrusts, bringing her along with him, higher and higher until he thought they would both shatter. Until he thought they might shatter everything in this room. All of these unbreakable, unbending things.

She lowered her head, her body going stiff as her release broke over her, her body spasming around his, that evidence of her own loss of control stealing every ounce of his own.

He gave himself up to this. Up to her. And when his climax hit him, it was with the realization that it was somehow hers. That she owned this. Owned this moment. Owned his body.

That realization only made it more intense. Only made it more arousing.

His muscles shook as he poured himself into her. As he gave himself up to it totally, completely, in a way he had given himself up to nothing and no one for more than five years. Maybe ever.

In this moment, surrounded by all of these creations that had come out of him, he was exposed, undone. As though he had ripped his chest open completely and exposed his every secret to her, as though she could see everything, not just these creations, but the ugly, secret things that he kept contained inside his soul.

It was enough to make his knees buckle, and he had to reach out, pressing his palm against the rough surface of the iron horse to keep himself from falling to the ground and dragging Maddy with him.

The only sound in the room was their broken breathing, fractured and unsteady. He gathered her up against his body, one hand against her stomach, the other still on the back of the horse, keeping them upright.

He angled his head, buried his face in her neck, kissed her.

"Well," Maddy said, her voice unsteady, "that was amazing."

He couldn't respond. Because he couldn't say anything. His tongue wasn't working; his brain wasn't working. His voice had dried up like a desert. Instead, he released his grip on the horse, turned her to face him and claimed her mouth in a deep, hard kiss.

Ten

Maybe it wasn't the best thing to make assumptions, but when they got back to Sam's house, that was exactly what Maddy did. She simply assumed that she would be invited inside because he wanted her to stay.

If her assumption was wrong, he didn't correct her.

She soaked in the details of his home, the simple, completely spare surroundings, and how it seemed to clash with his newfound wealth.

Except, in many ways it didn't, she supposed. Sam just didn't seem the type to go out and spend large. He was too…well, Sam.

The cabin was neat, well kept and small. Rustic and void of any kind of frills. Honestly, it was more rustic than the cabins they had stayed in up in the mountain.

It was just another piece that she could add to the Sam puzzle. He was such a strange man. So difficult to find the center of. To find the key to. He was one giant sheet of code and she was missing some essential bit that might help her make heads or tails of him.

He was rough; he was distant. He was caring and kinder in many ways than almost anyone else she had ever known. Certainly, he had listened to her in a way that no one else ever had before. Offering nothing and simply taking everything onto his shoulders, letting her feel whatever she did without telling her it was wrong.

That was valuable in a way that she hadn't realized it would be.

She wished that she could do the same for him. That she could figure out what the thing was that made Sam…Sam. That made him distant and difficult and a lot like a brick wall. But she knew there was more behind his aloofness. A potential for feeling, for emotion, that surpassed what he showed the world.

She didn't even bother to ask herself why she cared. She suspected she already knew.

Sam busied himself making a fire in the simple, old-fashioned fireplace in the living room. It was nothing like the massive, modern adorned piece that was in the West family living room. One with fake logs and a switch that turned it on. One with a mantel that boasted the various awards won by Nathan West's superior horses.

There was something about this that she liked. The lack of pretension. Though, she wondered if it reflected Sam any more honestly than her own home—decorated by her mother's interior designer—did her. She could see it, in a way. The fact that he was no-nonsense and a little bit spare.

And yet in other ways she couldn't.

His art pieces looked like they were ready to take a breath and come to life any moment. The fact that such beautiful things came out of him made her think there had to be beautiful things in him. An appreciation for aesthetics. And yet none of that was in evidence here. Of course, it would be an appreciation for a hard aesthetic, since there was nothing soft about what he did.

Still, he wasn't quite this cold and empty either.

Neither of them spoke while he stoked the fire, and pretty soon the small space began to warm. Her whole body was still buzzing with the aftereffects of what had happened in his studio. But still, she wanted more.

She hadn't intended to seduce him in his studio; it had just happened. But she didn't regret it. She had brought a condom, just in case, so she supposed she couldn't claim total innocence. But still.

It had been a little bit reckless. The kind of thing a person could get caught doing. It was definitely not as discreet as she should have been. The thought made her smile. Made her feel like Sam was washing away some of the wounds of her past. That he was healing her in a way she hadn't imagined she could be.

She walked over to where he was, still kneeling down in front of the fireplace, and she placed her hands on his shoulders. She felt his muscles tighten beneath her touch. All of the tension that he carried in his shoulders. Why? Because he wanted her again and that bothered him? It wasn't because he didn't want her, she was convinced of that. There was no faking what was between them.

She let her fingertips drift down lower. Then she leaned in, pressing a kiss to his neck, as he was so fond of doing to her. As she was so fond of him doing.

"What are you doing?" he asked, his voice rumbling inside him.

"Honestly, if you have to ask, I'm not doing a very good job of it."

"Aren't you exhausted?"

"The way I see it, I have five days left with you. I could go five days without sleep if I needed to."

He reached up, grabbing hold of her wrist and turning, then pulling her down onto the floor, onto his lap. "Is that a challenge? Because I'm more than up to meeting that."

"If you want to take it as one, I suppose that's up to you."

She put her hands on his face, sliding her thumbs alongside the grooves next to his mouth. He wasn't that old. In his early to midthirties, she guessed. But he wore some serious cares on that handsome face of his, etched into his skin. She wondered what they were. It was easy to assume it was the death of his parents, and perhaps that was part of it. But there was more.

She'd had the impression earlier today that she'd only ever glimpsed a small part of him. That there were deep pieces of himself that he kept concealed from the world. And she had a feeling this was one of them. That he was a man who presented himself as simple, who lived in these simple surroundings, hard and spare, while he contained multitudes of feeling and complexity.

She also had a feeling he would rather die than admit that.

"All right," he said, "if you insist."

He leaned in, kissing her. It was slower and more luxurious than any of the kisses they had shared back in the studio. A little bit less frantic. A little bit less desperate. Less driven toward its ultimate conclusion, much more about the journey.

She found herself being disrobed again, for the second time that day, and she really couldn't complain. Especially not when Sam joined her in a state of undress.

She pressed her hand against his chest, tracing the strongly delineated muscles, her eyes following the movement.

"I'm going to miss this," she said, not quite sure

what possessed her to speak the words out loud. Because they went so much deeper than just appreciation for his body. So much deeper than just missing his beautiful chest or his perfect abs.

She wished that they didn't, but they did. She wished she were a little more confused by the things she did and said with him, like she had been earlier today. But somehow, between her pouring her heart out to him at the ranch today and making love with him in the studio, a few things had become a lot clearer.

His lips twitched, like he was considering making light of the statement. Saying something to defuse the tension between them. Instead, he wrapped his fingers around her wrist, holding her tight, pressing her palms flat against him so that she could feel his heart beating. Then he kissed her. Long, powerful. A claiming, a complete and total invasion of her soul.

She didn't even care.

Or maybe, more accurately, she did care. She cared all the way down, and what she couldn't bother with anymore was all the pretending that she didn't. That she cared about nothing and no one, that she existed on the Isle of Maddy. Where she was wholly self-sufficient.

She was pretty sure, in this moment, that she might need him. That she might need him in ways she hadn't needed another person in a very long time, if ever. When she had met David, she had been a teenager. She hadn't had any baggage; she hadn't run into any kind of resistance in the world. She was young, and she didn't know what giving her heart away might cost.

She knew now. She knew so much more. She had been hurt; she had been broken. And when she allowed herself to see that she needed someone, she could see too just how badly it could go.

When they parted, they were both breathing hard, and his dark eyes were watchful on hers. She felt like she could see further than she normally could. Past all of that strength that he wore with ease, down to the parts of him that were scarred, that had been wounded.

That were vulnerable.

Even Sam McCormack was vulnerable. What a revelation. Perhaps if he was, everyone was.

He lifted his hand, brushing up against her cheek, down to her chin, and then he pushed her hair back off her face, slowly letting his fingers sift through the strands. And he watched them slide through his fingers, just as she had watched her own hand as she'd touched his chest. She wondered what he was thinking. If he was thinking what she'd been. If he was attached to her in spite of himself.

Part of her hoped so. Part of her hoped not.

He leaned down, kissing her on the shoulder, the seemingly nonsexual contact affecting her intensely. Making her skin feel like it was on fire, making her heart feel like it might burst right out of her chest.

She found herself being propelled backward, but it

felt like slow motion, as he lowered her down onto the floor. Onto the carpet there in front of the fireplace.

She had the thought that this was definitely a perfect component for a winter affair. But then the thought made her sad. Because she wanted so much more than a winter affair with him. So much more than this desperate grab in front of the fire, knowing that they had only five days left with each other.

But then he was kissing her and she couldn't think anymore. She couldn't regret. She could only kiss him back.

His hands skimmed over her curves, her breasts, her waist, her hips, all the way down to her thighs, where he squeezed her tight, held on to her as though she were his lifeline. As though he were trying to memorize every curve, every dip and swell.

She closed her eyes, gave herself over to it, to the sensation of being known by Sam. The thought filled her, made her chest feel like it was expanding. He knew her. He really knew her. And he was still here. Still with her. He didn't judge her; he didn't find her disgusting.

He didn't treat her like she was breakable. He could still bend her over a horse statue in his studio, then be like this with her in front of the fire. Tender. Sweet.

Because she was a woman who wanted both things. And he seemed to know it.

He also seemed to be a man who might need both too.

Or maybe everybody did. But you didn't see it until you were with the person you wanted to be both of those things with.

"Hang on just a second," he said, suddenly, breaking into her sensual reverie. She had lost track of time. Lost track of everything except the feel of his hands on her skin.

He moved away from her, the loss of his body leaving her cold. But he returned a moment later, settling himself in between her thighs. "Condom," he said by way of explanation.

At least one of them had been thinking. She certainly hadn't been.

He joined their bodies together, entering her slowly, the sensation of fullness, of being joined to him, suddenly so profound that she wanted to weep with it. It always felt good. From the first time with him it had felt good. But this was different.

It was like whatever veil had been between them, whatever stack of issues had existed, had been driving them, was suddenly dropped. And there was nothing between them. When he looked at her, poised over her, deep inside her, she felt like he could see all the way down.

When he moved, she moved with him, meeting him thrust for thrust, pushing them both to the brink. And when she came, he came along with her, his rough gasp of pleasure in her ears ramping up her own release.

In the aftermath, skin to skin, she couldn't deny

anymore what all these feelings were. She couldn't pretend that she didn't know.

She'd signed herself up for a twelve-day fling with a man she didn't even like, and only one week in she had gone and fallen in love with Sam McCormack.

"Sam." Maddy's voice broke into his sensual haze. He was lying on his back in front of the fireplace, feeling drained and like he had just had some kind of out-of-body experience. Except he had been firmly in his body and feeling everything, everything and then some.

"What?" he asked, his voice rusty.

"Why do you make farm animals?"

"What the hell kind of question is that?" he asked.

"A valid one," she said, moving nearer to him, putting her hand on his chest, tracing shapes there. "I mean, not that they aren't good."

"The horse seemed good enough for you a couple hours ago."

"It's good," she said, her tone irritated, because she obviously thought he was misunderstanding her on purpose.

Which she wasn't wrong about.

"Okay, but you don't think I should be making farm animals."

"No, I think it's fine that you make farm animals. I just think it's not actually you."

He shifted underneath her, trying to decide whether or not he should say anything. Or if he should sidestep the question. If it were anyone else, he would laugh. Play it off. Pretend like there was no answer. That there was nothing deeper in him than simply re-creating what he literally saw out in the fields in front of him.

And a lot of people would have bought that. His own brother probably would have, or at the very least, he wouldn't have pushed. But this was Maddy. Maddy, who had come apart in his arms in more than one way over the past week. Maddy, who perhaps saw deeper inside him than anyone else ever had.

Why not tell her? Why not? Because he could sense her getting closer to him. Could sense it like an invisible cord winding itself around the two of them, no matter that he was going to have to cut it in the end. Maybe it would be best to do it now.

"If I don't make what I see, I'll have to make what I feel," he said. "Nobody wants that."

"Why not?"

"Because the art has to sell," he said, his voice flat. Although, that was somewhat disingenuous. It wasn't that he didn't think he could sell darker pieces. In fact, he was sure that he could. "I don't do it for myself. I do it for Chase. I was perfectly content to keep it some kind of weird hobby that I messed around with after hours. Chase was the one who thought that I needed to pursue it full-time. Chase was the one who thought it was the way to save our business. And it started out doing kind of custom artistry for big houses. Gates and the detail work on stairs and decks and things. But then I started making bigger pieces and we started selling them. I say *we* because without Chase they would just sit in the shop."

"So you're just making what sells. That's the beginning and end of the story." Her blue eyes were too sharp, too insightful and far too close to the firelight for him to try to play at any games.

"I make what I want to let people see."

"What happened, Sam? And don't tell me nothing. You're talking to somebody who clung to one event in the past for as long as humanly possible. Who let it dictate her entire life. You're talking to the queen of residual issues here. Don't try to pretend that you don't have any. I know what it looks like." She took a deep breath. "I know what it looks like when somebody uses anger, spite and a whole bunch of unfriendliness to keep the world at a safe distance. I know, because I've spent the past ten years doing it. Nobody gets too close to the girl who says unpredictable things. The one who might come out and tell you that your dress does make you look fat and then turn around and say something crude about male anatomy. It's how you give yourself power in social situations. Act like you don't care about the rules that everyone else is a slave to." She laughed. "And why not? I already broke the rules. That's me. It's been me for a long time. And it isn't because I didn't know better. It's because I absolutely knew better. You're smart, Sam. The way that you walk around, the way you present yourself, even here, it's calculated."

Sam didn't think anyone had ever accused him of being calculated before. But it was true. Truer than most things that had been leveled at him. That he was grumpy, that he was antisocial. He was those things. But for a very specific reason.

And of course Madison would know. Of course she would see.

"I've never been comfortable sharing my life," Sam said. "I suppose that comes from having a father who was less than thrilled to have a son who was interested in art. In fact, I think my father considered it a moral failing of his. To have a son who wanted to use materials to create frivolous things. Things that had no use. To have a son who was more interested in that than honest labor. I learned to keep things to myself a long time ago. Which all sounds a whole lot like a sad, cliché story. Except it's not. It worked. I would have made a relationship with my dad work. But he died. So then it didn't matter anymore. But still, I just never... I never wanted to keep people up on what was happening with my life. I was kind of trained that way."

Hell, a lot of guys were that way, anyway. A lot of men didn't want to talk about what was happening in their day-to-day existence. Though most of them wouldn't have gone to the lengths that Sam did to keep everything separate.

"Most especially when Chase and I were neck-deep in trying to keep the business afloat, I didn't like him seeing that I was working on anything else. Anything at all." Sam took a deep breath. "That included any kind of relationships I might have. I didn't have a lot. But you know Chase never had a problem with people in town knowing that he was spreading it around. He never had a problem sleeping with the women here."

"No, he did not," Maddy said. "Never with me, to be clear."

"Considering I'm your first in a decade, I wasn't exactly that worried about it."

"Just making sure."

"I didn't like that. I didn't want my life to be part of this real-time small-town TV program. I preferred to find women out of town. When I was making deliveries, going to bigger ranches down the coast, that was when I would…"

"When you would find yourself a buckle bunny for the evening?"

"Yes," he said. "Except I met a woman I liked a lot. She was the daughter of one of the big ranchers down near Coos County. And I tried to keep things business oriented. We were actually doing business with her family. But I…I saw her out at a bar one night, and even though I knew she was too young, too nice of a girl for a guy like me…I slept with her. And a few times after. I was pretty obsessed with her, actually."

He was downplaying it. But what was the point

of doing anything else? Of admitting that for just a little while he'd thought he'd found something. Someone who wanted him. All of him. Someone who knew him.

The possibility of a future. Like the first hint of spring in the air after a long winter.

Maddy moved closer to him, looking up at him, and he decided to take a moment to enjoy that for a second. Because after this, she would probably never want to touch him again.

"Without warning, she cut me off. Completely. Didn't want to see me anymore. And since she was a few hours down the highway, that really meant not seeing her. I'd had to make an effort to work her into my life. Cutting her out of it was actually a lot easier."

"Sure," Maddy said, obviously not convinced.

"I got a phone call one night. Late. From the hospital. They told me to come down because Elizabeth was asking for me. They said it wasn't good."

"Oh, Sam," Maddy said, her tone tinged with sympathy.

He brush right past that. Continued on. "I white-knuckled it down there. Went as fast as I could. I didn't tell anyone I was going. When I got there, they wouldn't let me in. Because I wasn't family."

"But she wanted them to call you."

"It didn't matter." It was difficult for him to talk about that day. In fact, he never had. He could see it all playing out in his mind as he spoke the words.

Could see the image of her father walking out of the double doors, looking harried, older than Sam had ever seen him look during any of their business dealings.

"I never got to see her," Sam said. "She died a few minutes after I got there."

"Sam, I'm so sorry..."

"No, don't misunderstand me. This isn't a story about me being angry because I lost a woman that I loved. I *didn't* love her. That's the worst part." He swallowed hard, trying to diffuse the pressure in his throat crushing down, making it hard to breathe. "I mean, maybe I could have. But that's not the same. You know who loved her? Her family. Her family loved her. I have never seen a man look so destroyed as I did that day. Looking at her father, who clearly wondered why in hell I was sitting down there in the emergency room. Why I had been called to come down. He didn't have to wonder long. Not when they told him exactly how his daughter died." Sam took a deep breath. "Elizabeth died of internal bleeding. Complications from an ectopic pregnancy."

Maddy's face paled, her lips looking waxen. "Did you...? You didn't know she was pregnant."

"No. Neither did anyone in her family. But I know it was mine. I know it was mine, and she didn't want me to know. And that was probably why she didn't tell me, why she broke things off with me. Nobody knew because she was ashamed. Because it was my baby. Because it was a man that she knew she couldn't have a future with. Nobody knew, so when she felt tired and lay down for a nap because she was bleeding and feeling discomfort, no one was there."

Silence settled around them, the house creaking beneath the weight of it.

"Did you ever find out why...why she called you then?"

"I don't know. Maybe she wanted me there to blame me. Maybe she just needed me. I'll never know. She was gone before I ever got to see her."

"That must have been..." Maddy let that sentence trail off. "That's horrible."

"It's nothing but horrible. It's everything horrible. I know why she got pregnant, Maddy. It's because... I was so careless with her. I had sex with her once without a condom. And I thought that it would be fine. Hell, I figured if something did happen, I'd be willing to marry her. All of that happened because I didn't think. Because I lost control. I don't deserve..."

"You can't blame yourself for a death that was some kind of freak medical event."

"Tell me you wouldn't blame yourself, Maddy. Tell me you wouldn't." He sat up, and Maddy sat up too. Then he gripped her shoulders, holding her steady, forcing her to meet his gaze. "You, who blame yourself for the affair with your dressage teacher even though you were an underage girl. You could tell me you don't. You could tell me that you were just hurt by the way everybody treated you, but

I know it's more than that. You blame yourself. So don't you dare look at me with those wide blue eyes and tell me that I have no business blaming myself."

She blinked. "I…I don't blame myself. I don't. I mean, I'm not proud of what I did, but I'm not going to take all of the blame. Not for something I couldn't control. He lied to me. I was dumb, yes. I was naive. But dammit, Sam, my father should have had my back. My friends should have had my back. And my teacher should never have taken advantage of me."

He moved away from her then, pushing himself into a standing position and forking his fingers through his hair. She wasn't blaming him. It was supposed to push her away. She certainly wasn't supposed to look at him with sympathy. She was supposed to be appalled. Appalled that he had taken the chances he had with Elizabeth's body. Appalled at his lack of control.

It was the object lesson. The one that proved that he wasn't good enough for a woman like her. That he wasn't good enough for anyone.

"You don't blame yourself at all?"

"I don't know," she said. "It's kind of a loaded question. I could have made another decision. And because of that, I guess I share blame. But I'm not going to sit around feeling endless guilt. I'm hurt. I'm wounded. But that's not the same thing. Like I told you, the sex was the least of it. If it was all guilt, I would have found somebody a long time ago. I would have dealt with it. But it's more than that. I think it's more than that with you. Because you're not an idiot. You know full well that it isn't like you're the first man to have unprotected sex with a woman. You know full well you weren't in control of where an embryo implanted inside a woman. You couldn't have taken her to the hospital, because you didn't know she was pregnant. You didn't know she needed you. She sent you away. She made some choices here, and I don't really think it's her fault either, because how could she have known? But still. It isn't your fault."

He drew back, anger roaring through him. "I'm the one…"

"You're very dedicated to this. But that doesn't make it true."

"Her father thought it was my fault," he said. "That matters. I had to look at a man who was going to have to bury his daughter because of me."

"Maybe he felt that way," Maddy said. "I can understand that. People want to blame. I know. Because I've been put in that position. Where I was the one that people wanted to blame. Because I wasn't as well liked. Because I wasn't as important. I know that David's wife certainly wanted to blame me, because she wanted to make her marriage work, and if she blamed David, how would she do that? And without blame, your anger is aimless."

Those words hit hard, settled somewhere down deep inside him. And he knew that no matter what, no matter that he didn't want to think about them, no matter that he didn't want to believe them, they were going to stay with him. Truth had a funny way of doing that.

"I'm not looking for absolution, Maddy." He shook his head. "I was never looking for it."

"What are you looking for, then?"

He shrugged. "Nothing. I'm not looking for anything. I'm not looking for you to forgive me. I'm not looking to forgive myself."

"No," she said, "you're just looking to keep punishing yourself. To hold everything inside and keep it buried down deep. I don't think it's the rest of the world you're hiding yourself from. I think you're hiding from yourself."

"You think that you are qualified to talk about my issues? You. The woman who didn't have a lover for ten years because she's so mired in the past?"

"Do you think that's going to hurt my feelings? I know I'm messed up. I'm well aware. In fact, I would argue that it takes somebody as profoundly screwed up as I am to look at another person and see it. Maybe other people would look at you and see a man who is strong. A man who has it all laid out. A man who has iron control. But I see you for what you are. You're completely and totally bound up inside. And you're ready to crack apart. You can't go on like this."

"Watch me," he said.

"How long has it been?" she asked, her tone soft.

"Five years," he ground out.

"Well, it's only half the time I've been punishing myself, but it's pretty good. Where do you see it ending, Sam?"

"Well, you were part of it for me too."

He gritted his teeth, regretting introducing that revelation into the conversation.

"What do you mean?"

"I haven't been with a woman in five years. So I guess you could say you are part of me dealing with some of my issues."

Maddy looked like she'd been slapped. She did not, in any way, look complimented. "What does that mean? What does that mean?" She repeated the phrase twice, sounding more horrified, more frantic each time.

"It had to end at some point. The celibacy, I mean. And when you offered yourself, I wasn't in a position to say no."

"After all of your righteous indignation—the accusation that I was using you for sexual healing—it turns out you were using me for the same thing?" she asked.

"Why does that upset you so much?"

"Because…because you're still so completely wrapped up in it. Because you obviously don't have any intention to really be healed."

Unease settled in his chest. "What's me being healed to you, Maddy? What does that mean? I changed something, didn't I? Same as you."

"But…" Her tone became frantic. "I just… You aren't planning on letting it change you."

"What change are you talking about?" he pressed.

"I don't know," she said, her throat sounding constricted.

"Like hell, Madison. Don't give me that. If you've changed the rules in your head, that's hardly my fault."

She whirled around, lowering her head, burying her face in her hands. "You're so infuriating." She turned back to him, her cheeks crimson. "I don't know what either of us was thinking. That we were going to go into this and come out the other side without changing anything? We are idiots. We are idiots who didn't let another human being touch us for years. And somehow we thought we could come together and nothing would change? I mean, it was one thing when it was just me. I assumed that you went around having sex with women you didn't like all the time."

"Why would you think that?"

"Because you don't like anyone. So, that stands to reason. That you would sleep with women you don't like. I certainly didn't figure you didn't sleep with women at all. That's ridiculous. You're... *Look* at you. Of course you have sex. Who would assume that you didn't? Not me. That's who."

He gritted his teeth, wanting desperately to redirect the conversation. Because it was going into territory that would end badly for both of them. He wanted to leave the core of the energy arcing between them unspoken. He wanted to make sure that neither of them acknowledged it. He wanted to pretend he had no idea what she was thinking. No idea what she was about to say.

The problem was, he knew her. Better than he knew anyone else, maybe. And it had all happened in a week. A week of talking, of being skin to skin. Of being real.

No wonder he had spent so many years avoiding exactly this. No wonder he had spent so long hiding everything that he was, everything that he wanted. Because the alternative was letting it hang out there, exposed and acting as some kind of all-access pass to anyone who bothered to take a look.

"Well, you assumed wrong. But it doesn't have to change anything. We have five more days, Maddy. Why does it have to be like this?"

"Honest?"

"Why do we have to fight with each other? We shouldn't. We don't have to. We don't have to continue this discussion. We are not going to come to any kind of understanding, whatever you might think. Whatever you think you're pushing for here… just don't."

"Are you going to walk away from this and just not change? Are you going to find another woman? Is that all this was? A chance for you to get your sexual mojo back? To prove that you could use a condom every time? Did you want me to sew you a little sexual merit badge for your new Boy Scout vest?" She let out a frustrated growl. "I don't want you to be a Boy Scout, Sam. I want you to be you."

Sam growled, advancing on her. She backed away from him until her shoulder blades hit the wall. Then he pressed his palms to the flat surface on either side of her face. "You don't want me to be me. Trust me. I don't know how to give the kinds of things you want."

"You don't want to," she said, the words soft, penetrating deeper than a shout ever could have.

"No, you don't want me to."

"Why is that so desperately important for you to make yourself believe?"

"Because it's true."

She let silence hang between them for a moment. "Why won't you let yourself feel this?"

"What?"

"*This* is why you do farm animals. That's what you said. And you said it was because nobody would want to see this. But that isn't true. Everybody feels grief, Sam. Everybody has lost. Plenty of people would want to see what you would make from this. Why is it that you can't do it?"

"You want me to go ahead and make a profit off my sins? Out of the way I hurt other people? You want me to make some kind of artistic homage to a father who never wanted me to do art in the first place? You want me to do a tribute to a woman whose death I contributed to."

"Yes. Because it's not about how anyone else feels. It's about how you feel."

He didn't know why this reached in and cut him so deeply. He didn't know why it bothered him so much. Mostly he didn't know why he was having this conversation with her at all. It didn't change anything. It didn't change him.

"No," she said, "that isn't what I think you should do. It's not about profiting off sins—real or perceived. It's about you dealing with all of these things. It's about you acknowledging that you have feelings."

He snorted. "I'm entitled to more grief than Elizabeth's parents? To any?"

"You lost somebody that you cared about. That matters. Of course it matters. You lost... I don't know. She was pregnant. It was your baby. Of course that matters. Of course you think about it."

"No," he said, the words as flat as everything inside him. "I don't. I don't think about that. Ever. I don't talk about it. I don't do anything with it."

"Except make sure you never make a piece of art that means anything to you. Except not sleep with anyone. Except punish yourself. Which you had such a clear vision of when you felt like I was doing it to myself but you seem to be completely blind to when it comes to you."

"All right. Let's examine your mistake, then, Maddy. Since you're so determined to draw a comparison between the two of us. Who's dead? Come on. Who died as a result of your youthful mistakes?

No one. Until you make a mistake like that, something that's that irreversible, don't pretend you have any idea what I've been through. Don't pretend you have any idea of what I should feel."

He despised himself for even saying that. For saying he had been through something. He didn't deserve to walk around claiming that baggage. It was why he didn't like talking about it. It was why he didn't like thinking about it. Because Elizabeth's family members were the ones who had been left with a giant hole in their lives. Not him. Because they were the ones who had to deal with her loss around the dinner table, with thinking about her on her birthday and all of the holidays they didn't have her.

He didn't even know when her birthday was.

"Well, I care about you," Maddy said, her voice small. "Doesn't that count for anything?"

"No," he said, his voice rough. "Five more days, Maddy. That's it. That's all it can ever be."

He should end it now. He knew that. Beyond anything else, he knew that he should end it now. But if Maddy West had taught him anything, it was that he wasn't nearly as controlled as he wanted to be. At least, not where she was concerned. He could stand around and shout about it, self-flagellate all he wanted, but when push came to shove, he was going to make the selfish decision.

"Either you come to bed with me and we spend the rest of the night not talking, or you go home and we can forget the rest of this."

Maddy nodded mutely. He expected her to turn and walk out the door. Maybe not even pausing to collect her clothes, in spite of the cold weather. Instead, she surprised him. Instead, she took his hand, even knowing the kind of devastation it had caused, and she turned and led him up the stairs.

Eleven

Maddy hadn't slept at all. It wasn't typical for her and Sam to share a bed the entire night. But they had last night. After all that shouting and screaming and lovemaking, it hadn't seemed right to leave. And he hadn't asked her to.

She knew more about him now than she had before. In fact, she had a suspicion that she knew everything about him. Even if it wasn't all put together into a complete picture. It was there. And now, with the paie morning light filtering through the window, she was staring at him as though she could make it all form a cohesive image.

As if she could will herself to somehow understand what all of those little pieces meant. As if she could make herself see the big picture.

Sam couldn't even see it, of that she was certain. So she had no idea how she could expect herself to see it. Except that she wanted to. Except that she needed to. She didn't want to leave him alone with all of that. It was too much. It was too much for any one man. He felt responsible for the death of that woman. Or at least, he was letting himself think he did.

Protecting himself. Protecting himself with pain.

It made a strange kind of sense to her, only because she was a professional at protecting herself. At insulating herself from whatever else might come her way. Yes, it was a solitary existence. Yes, it was lonely. But there was control within that. She had a feeling that Sam operated in much the same way.

She shifted, brushing his hair out of his face. He had meant to frighten her off. He had given her an out. And she knew that somehow he had imagined she would take it. She knew that he believed he was some kind of monster. At least, part of him believed it.

Because she could also tell that he had been genuinely surprised that she hadn't turned tail and run.

But she hadn't. And she wouldn't. Mostly because she was just too stubborn. She had spent the past ten years being stubborn. Burying who she was underneath a whole bunch of bad attitude and sharp words. Not letting anyone get close, even though she had a bunch of people around her who cared. She had chosen to focus on the people who didn't. The people who didn't care enough. While simultaneously deciding that the people who did care enough, who cared more than enough, somehow weren't as important.

Well, she was done with that. There were people in her life who loved her. Who loved her no matter what. And she had a feeling that Sam had the ability to be one of those people. She didn't want to abandon him to this. Not when he had—whether he would admit it or not—been instrumental in digging her out of her self-imposed emotional prison.

"Good morning," she whispered, pressing her lips to his cheek.

As soon as she did that, a strange sense of foreboding stole over her. As though she knew that the next few moments were going to go badly. But maybe that was just her natural pessimism. The little beast she had built up to be the strongest and best-developed piece of her. Another defense.

Sam's eyes opened, and the shock that she glimpsed there absolutely did not bode well for the next few moments. She knew that. "I stayed the night," she said, in response to the unasked question she could see lurking on his face.

"I guess I fell asleep," he said, his voice husky.

"Clearly." She took a deep breath. Oh well. If it was all going to hell, it might as well go in style. "I want you to come to the family Christmas party with me."

It took only a few moments for her to decide that she was going to say those words. And that she was going to follow them up with everything that was brimming inside her. Feelings that she didn't feel like keeping hidden. Not anymore. Maybe it was selfish. But she didn't really care. She knew his stuff. He knew hers. The only excuse she had for not telling him how she felt was self-protection.

She knew where self-protection got her. Absolutely nowhere. Treading water in a stagnant pool of her own failings, never advancing any further on in her life. In her existence. It left her lonely. It left her without any real, true friends. She didn't want that. Not anymore. And if she had to allow herself to be wounded in the name of authenticity, in the name of trying again, then she would.

An easy decision to make before the injury occurred. But it was made nonetheless.

"Why?" Sam asked, rolling away from her, getting up out of bed.

She took that opportunity to drink in every detail of his perfect body. His powerful chest, his muscular thighs. Memorizing every little piece of him. More Sam for her collection. She had a feeling that eventually she would walk away from him with nothing but that collection. A little pail full of the shadows of what she used to have.

"Because I would like to have a date." She was stalling now.

"You want to make your dad mad? Is that what we're doing? A little bit of revenge for everything he put you through?"

"I would never use you that way, Sam. I hope you know me better than that."

"We don't know each other, Maddy. We don't. We've had a few conversations, and we've had some sex. But that doesn't mean knowing somebody. Not really."

"That just isn't true. Nobody else knows how I feel about what happened to me. Nobody. Nobody else knows about the conversation I had with my dad. And I would imagine that nobody knows about Elizabeth. Not the way that I do."

"We used each other as a confessional. That isn't the same."

"The funny thing is it did start that way. At least for me. Because what did it matter what you knew. We weren't going to have a relationship after. So I didn't have to worry about you judging me. I didn't have to worry about anything."

"And?"

"That was just what I told myself. It was what made it feel okay to do what I wanted to do. We lie to ourselves. We get really deep in it when we feel like we need protection. That was what I was doing. But the simple truth is I felt a connection with you from the beginning. It was why I was so terrible to you. Because it scared me."

"You should have kept on letting it scare you, baby girl."

Those words acted like a shot of rage that went straight to her stomach, then fired onto her head.

"Why? Because it's the thing that allows you to maintain your cranky-loner mystique? That isn't you. I thought maybe you didn't feel anything. But now I think you feel everything. And it scares you. I'm the same way."

"I see where this is going, Maddy. Don't do it. Don't. I can tell you right now it isn't going to go the way you think it will."

"Oh, go ahead, Sam. Tell me what I think. Please. I'm dying to hear it."

"You think that because you've had some kind of transformation, some kind of deep realization, that I'm headed for the same. But it's bullshit. I'm sorry to be the one to tell you. Wishful thinking on a level I never wanted you to start thinking on. You knew the rules. You knew them from the beginning."

"Don't," she said, her throat tightening, her chest constricting. "Don't do this to us. Don't pretend it can stay the same thing it started out as. Because it isn't. And you know it."

"You're composing a really compelling story, Madison." The reversion back to her full name felt significant. "And we both know that's something you do. Make more out of sex than it was supposed to be."

She gritted her teeth, battling through. Because he wanted her to stop. He wanted this to intimidate, to hurt. He wanted it to stop her. But she wasn't going to let him win. Not at this. Not at his own self-destruction. "Jackass 101. Using somebody's deep pain against them. I thought you were above that, Sam."

"It turns out I'm not. You might want to pay attention to that."

"I'm paying attention. I want you to come with me to the Christmas party, Sam. Because I want it to be the beginning. I don't want it to be the end."

"Don't do this."

He bent down, beginning to collect his clothes, his focus on anything in the room but her. She took a deep breath, knowing that what happened next was going to shatter all of this.

"I need more. I need more than twelve days of Christmas. I want it every day. I want to wake up with you every morning and go to bed with you every night. I want to fight with you. I want to make love with you. I want to tell you my secrets. To show you every dark, hidden thing in me. The serious things and the silly things. Because I love you. It's that complicated and that simple. I love you and that means I'm willing to do this, no matter how it ends."

Sam tugged his pants on, did them up, then pulled his shirt over his head. "I told you not to do this, Maddy. But you're doing it anyway. And you know what that makes it? A suicide mission. You stand there, thinking you're being brave because you're telling the truth. But you know how it's going to end. You know that after you make this confession, you're not actually going to have to deal with the relationship with me, because I already told you it isn't happening. I wonder if you would have been so brave if you knew I might turn around and offer you forever."

His words hit her with the force of bullets. But for some reason, they didn't hurt. Not really. She could remember distinctly when David had broken things off with her. Saying that she had never been anything serious. That she had been only a little bit of tail on the side and he was of course going to have to stay with his wife. Because she was the center of his life. Of his career. Because she mattered, and Maddy didn't. That had hurt. It had hurt because it had been true.

Because David hadn't loved her. And it had been easy for him to break up with her because he had never intended on having more with her, and not a single part of him wanted more.

This was different. It was different because Sam was trying to hurt her out of desperation. Because Sam was lying. Or at the very least, was sidestepping. Because he didn't want to have the conversation.

Because he would have to lie to protect himself. Because he couldn't look her in the eye and tell her that he didn't love her, that she didn't matter.

But she wasn't certain he would let himself feel it. That was the gamble. She knew he felt it. She knew it. That deep down, Sam cared. She wasn't sure if he knew it. If he had allowed himself access to those feelings. Feelings that Sam seemed to think were a luxury, or a danger. Grief. Desire. Love.

"Go ahead and offer it. You won't. You won't, because you know I would actually say yes. You can try to make this about how damaged I am, but all of this is because of you."

"You have to be damaged to want somebody like me. You know what's in my past."

"Grief. Grief that you won't let yourself feel. Sadness you don't feel like you're allowed to have. That's what's in your past. Along with lost hope. Let's not pretend you blame yourself. You felt so comfortable calling me out, telling me that I was playing games. Well, guess what. That's what you're doing. You think if you don't want anything, if you don't need anything, you won't be hurt again. But you're just living in hurt and that isn't better."

"You have all this clarity about your own emotional situation, and you think that gives you a right to talk about mine?"

She threw the blankets off her and got out of bed. "Why not?" she asked, throwing her arms wide. She didn't care that she was naked. In fact, in many ways it seemed appropriate. That Sam had put clothes on, that he had felt the need to cover himself, and that she didn't even care anymore. She had no pride left. But this wasn't about pride.

"You think you have the right to talk about mine," she continued. "You think you're going to twist everything that I'm saying and eventually you'll find some little doubt inside me that will make me believe you're telling the truth. I've had enough of that. I've had enough of men telling me what I feel. Of them telling me what I should do. I'm not going to let you do it. You're better than that. At least, I thought you were."

"Maybe I'm not."

"Right now? I think you don't want to be. But I would love you through this too, Sam. You need to know that. You need to know that whatever you say right now, in this room, it's not going to change the way that I feel about you. You don't have that kind of power."

"That's pathetic. There's nothing I can say to make you not love me? Why don't you love yourself a little bit more than that, Madison," he said, his tone hard.

And regardless of what she had just said, that did hit something in her. Something vulnerable and scared. Something that was afraid she really hadn't learned how to be anything more than a pathetic creature, desperate for a man to show her affection.

"I love myself just enough to put myself out there and demand this," she said finally, her voice vibrating with conviction. "I love myself too much to slink off silently. I love myself too much not to fight for what I know we could have. If I didn't do this, if I didn't say this, it would only be for my pride. It would be so I could score points and feel like maybe I won. But in the end, if I walk away without having fought for you with everything I have in me, we will have both lost. I think you're worth that. I know you are. Why don't you think so?"

"Why do you?" he asked, his voice thin, brittle. "I don't think I've shown you any particular kindness or tenderness."

"Don't. Don't erase everything that's happened between us. Everything I told you. Everything you gave me."

"Keeping my mouth shut while I held a beautiful woman and let her talk? That's easy."

"I love you, Sam. That's all. I'm not going to stand here and have an argument. I'm not going to let you get in endless barbs while you try to make those words something less than true. I love you. I would really like it if you could tell me you loved me too."

"I don't." His words were flat in the room. And she knew they were all she would get from him. Right now, it was all he could say. And he believed it. He believed it down to his bones. That he didn't love her. That everything that had taken place between them over the past week meant nothing. Because he had to. Because behind that certainty, that flat, horrifying expression in his eyes, was fear.

Strong, beautiful Sam, who could bend iron to his will, couldn't overpower the fear that lived inside him. And she would never be able to do it for him.

"Okay," she said softly, beginning to gather her clothes. She didn't know how to do this. She didn't know what to do now. How to make a triumphant exit. So she decided she wouldn't. She decided to let the tears fall down her cheeks; she decided not to make a joke. She decided not to say anything flip-pant or amusing.

Because that was what the old Maddy would have done. She would have played it off. She would have tried to laugh. She wouldn't have let herself feel this, not all the way down. She wouldn't have let her heart feel bruised or tender. Wouldn't have let a wave of pain roll over her. Wouldn't have let herself feel it, not really.

And when she walked out of his house, sniffling, her shoulders shaking, and could no longer hold back the sob that was building in her chest by the time she reached her car, she didn't care. She didn't feel ashamed.

There was no shame in loving someone.

She opened the driver-side door and sat down. And then the dam burst. She had loved so many peo-ple who had never loved her in return. Not the way she loved them. She had made herself hard because of it. She had put the shame on her own shoulders.

That somehow a seventeen-year-old girl should have known that her teacher was lying to her. That somehow a daughter whose father had walked her down Main Street and bought her sweets in a little shop should have known that her father's affection had its limits.

That a woman who had met a man who had finally reached deep inside her and moved all those defenses she had erected around her heart should have known that in the end he would break it.

No. It wasn't her. It wasn't the love that was bad. It was the pride. The shame. The fear. Those were the things that needed to be gotten rid of.

She took a deep, shaking breath. She blinked hard, forcing the rest of her tears to fall, and then she started the car.

She would be okay. Because she had found herself again. Had learned how to love again. Had found a deep certainty and confidence in herself that had been missing for so long.

But as she drove away, she still felt torn in two. Because while she had been made whole, she knew that she was leaving Sam behind, still as broken as she had found him.

Twelve

Sam thought he might be dying. But then, that could easily be alcohol poisoning. He had been drinking and going from his house into his studio for the past two days. And that was it. He hadn't talked to anyone. He had nothing to say. He had sent Maddy away, and while he was firmly convinced it was the only thing he could have done, it hurt like a son of a bitch.

It shouldn't. It had been necessary. He couldn't love her the way that she wanted him to. He couldn't. There was no way in hell. Not a man like him.

Her words started to crowd in on him unbidden, the exact opposite thing that he wanted to remember right now. About how there was no point blaming himself. About how that wasn't the real issue. He growled, grabbing hold of the hammer he'd been using and flinging it across the room. It landed in a pile of scrap metal, the sound satisfying, the lack of damage unsatisfying.

He had a fire burning hot, and the room was stifling. He stripped his shirt off, feeling like he couldn't catch his breath. He felt like he was losing his mind. But then, he wasn't a stranger to it. He had felt this way after his parents had died. Again after Elizabeth. There was so much inside him, and there was nowhere for it to go.

And just like those other times, he didn't deserve this pain. Not at all. He was the one who had hurt her. He was the one who couldn't stand up to that declaration of love. He didn't deserve this pain.

But no matter how deep he tried to push it down, no matter how he tried to pound it out with a hammer, it still remained. And his brain was blank. He couldn't even figure out how the hell he might fashion some of this material into another cow.

It was like the thing inside him that told him how to create things had left along with Maddy.

He looked over at the bottle of Jack Daniel's that was sitting on his workbench. And cursed when he saw that it was empty. He was going to have to get more. But he wasn't sure he had more in the house. Which meant leaving the house. Maybe going to Chase's place and seeing if there was anything to take. Between that and sobriety it was a difficult choice.

He looked around, looked at the horse that he had

bent Maddy over just three days ago. Everything seemed dead now. Cold. Dark. Usually he felt the life in the things that he made. Something he would never tell anyone, because it sounded stupid. Because it exposed him.

But it was like Maddy had come in here and changed things. Taken everything with her when she left.

He walked over to the horse, braced his hands on the back of it and leaned forward, giving into the wave of pain that crashed over him suddenly, uncontrollably.

"I thought I might find you in here."

Sam lifted his head at the sound of his brother's voice. "I'm busy."

"Right. Which is why there is nothing new in here, but it smells flammable."

"I had a drink."

"Or twelve," Chase said, sounding surprisingly sympathetic. "If you get too close to that forge, you're going to burst into flame."

"That might not be so bad."

"What's going on? You're always a grumpy bastard, but this is different. You don't usually disappear for days at a time. Actually, I can pick up a couple of times that you've done that in the past. You usually reemerge worse and even more impossible than you were before. So if that is what's happening here, I would appreciate a heads-up."

"It's nothing. Artistic temper tantrum."

"I don't believe that." Chase crossed his arms and leaned against the back wall of the studio, making it very clear that he intended to stay until Sam told him something.

Fine. The bastard could hang out all day for all he cared. It didn't mean he had to talk.

"Believe whatever you want," Sam said. "But it's not going to make hanging out here any more interesting. I can't figure out what to make next. Are you happy? I have no idea. I have no inspiration." Suddenly, everything in him boiled over. "And I hate that. I hate that it matters. I should just be able to think of something to do. Or not care if I don't want to do it. But somehow, I can't make it work if I don't care at least a little bit. I hate caring, Chase. I *hate* it."

He hated it for every damn thing. Every damn, fragile thing.

"I know," Chase said. "And I blame Dad for that. He didn't understand. That isn't your fault. And it's not your flaw that you care. Think about the way he was about ranching. It was ridiculous. Weather that didn't go his way would send him into some kind of emotional tailspin for weeks. And he felt the same way about iron that you do. It's just that he felt compelled to shape it into things that had a function. But he took pride in his work. And he was an artist with it—you know he was. If anything, I think he was shocked by what you could do. Maybe even a little bit jealous. And he didn't know what to do with it."

Sam resisted those words. And the truth in them. "It doesn't matter."

"It does. Because it's why you can't talk about what you do. It's why you don't take pride in it the way that you should. It's why you're sitting here downplaying the fact you're having some kind of art block when it's been pretty clear for a few months that you have been."

"It shouldn't be a thing."

Chase shrugged. "Maybe not. But the very thing that makes your work valuable is also what makes it difficult. You're not a machine."

Sam wished he was. More than anything, he wished that he was. So that he wouldn't care about a damn thing. So that he wouldn't care about Maddy.

Softness, curves, floated to the forefront of his mind. Darkness and grief. All the inspiration he could ever want. Except that he couldn't take it. It wasn't his. He didn't own it. None of it.

He was still trying to pull things out of his own soul, and all he got was dry, hard work that looked downright ugly to him.

"I should be," he said, stubborn.

"This isn't about Dad, though. I don't even think it's about the art, though I think it's related. There was a woman, wasn't there?"

Sam snorted. "When?"

"Recently. Like the past week. Mostly I think so because I recognize that all-consuming obsession. Because I recognize this. Because you came and kicked my ass when I was in a very similar position just a year ago. And you know what you told me? With great authority, you told me that iron had to get hot to get shaped into something. You told me that I was in my fire, and I had to let it shape me into the man Anna needed me to be."

"Yeah, I guess I did tell you that," Sam said.

"Obviously I'm not privy to all the details of your personal life, Sam, which is your prerogative. But you're in here actively attempting to drink yourself to death. You say that you can't find any inspiration for your art. I would say that you're in a pretty damn bad situation. And maybe you need to pull yourself out of it. If that means grabbing hold of her—whoever she is—then do it."

Sam felt like the frustration inside him was about to overflow. "I can't. There's too much… There's too much. If you knew, Chase. If you knew everything about me, you wouldn't think I deserved it."

"Who deserves it?" Chase asked. "Does anybody? Do you honestly think I deserve Anna? I don't. But I love her. And I work every day to deserve her. It's a work in progress, let me tell you. But that's love. You just kind of keep working for it."

"There are too many other things in the way," Sam said, because he didn't know how else to articulate it. Without having a confessional, here in his studio, he didn't know how else to have this conversation.

"What things? What are you afraid of, Sam? Having a feeling? Is that what all this is about? The fact you want to protect yourself? The fact that it matters more to you that you get to keep your stoic expression and your who-gives-a-damn attitude intact?"

"It isn't that. It's never been that. But how—" He started again. "How was I supposed to grieve for Dad when you lost your mentor? How was I supposed to grieve for Mom when you were so young? It wasn't fair." And how the hell was he supposed to grieve for Elizabeth, for the child he didn't even know she had been carrying, when her own family was left with nothing.

"Of course you could grieve for them. They were your parents."

"Somebody has to be strong, Chase."

"And you thought I was weak? You think somehow grieving for my parents was weak?"

"Of course not. But... I was never the man that Dad wanted me to be. Now when he was alive. I didn't do what he wanted me to do. I didn't want the things that he wanted."

"Neither did I. And we both just about killed ourselves working this place the way that he wanted us to while it slowly sank into the ground. Then we had to do things on our terms. Because actually, we did know what we were talking about. And who we are, the gifts that we have, those mattered. If it wasn't for the fact that I have a business mind, if it wasn't for the fact that you could do the artwork, the ranch wouldn't be here. McCormack Ironworks wouldn't exist. And if Dad had lived, he would be proud of us. Because in the end we saved this place."

"I just don't... I had a girlfriend who died." He didn't know why he had spoken the words. He hadn't intended to. "She wasn't my girlfriend when she died. But she bled to death. At the hospital. She had been pregnant. And it was mine."

Chase cursed and fell back against the wall, bracing himself. "Seriously?"

"Yes. And I want... I want to do something with that feeling. But her family is devastated, Chase. They lost so much more than I did. And I don't know how... I don't know what to do with all of this. I don't know what to do with all of these feelings. I don't feel like I deserve them. I don't feel like I deserve the pain. Not in the way that I deserve to walk away from it unscathed. But I feel like it isn't mine. Like I'm taking something from them, or making something about me that just shouldn't be. But it's there all the same. And it follows me around. And Maddy loves me. She said she loves me. And I don't know how to take that either."

"Bullshit," Chase said, his voice rough. "That's not it."

"Don't tell me how it is, Chase, not when you don't know."

"Of course I know, Sam. Loss is hell. And I didn't lose half of what you did."

"It was just the possibility of something. Elizabeth. It wasn't... It was just..."

"Sam. You lost your parents. And a woman you were involved with who was carrying your baby. Of course you're screwed up. But walking around pretending you're just grumpy, pretending you don't want anything, that you don't care about anything, doesn't protect you from pain. It's just letting fear poison you from the inside."

Sam felt like he was staring down into an abyss that had no end. A yawning, bottomless cavern that was just full of need. All the need he had ever felt his entire life. The words ricocheted back at him, hit him like shrapnel, damaging, wounding. They were the truth. That it was what drove him, that it was what stopped him.

Fear.

That it was why he had spent so many years hiding.

And as blindingly clear as it was, it was also clear that Maddy was right about him. More right about him than he'd ever been about himself.

That confession made him think of Maddy too. Of the situation she was in with her father. Of those broken words she had spoken to him about how if her own father didn't think she was worth defending, who would? And he had sent her away, like he didn't think she was worth it either. Like he didn't think she was worth the pain or the risk.

Except he did. He thought she was worth defending. That she was worth loving. That she was worth everything.

Sam felt... Well, nothing on this earth had ever

made him feel small before. But this did it. He felt
scared. He felt weak. Mostly he felt a kind of over-
whelming sadness for everything he'd lost. For all
the words that were left unsaid. The years of grief
that had built up.

It had never been about control. It had never been
based in reality. Or about whether or not he deserved
something. Not really. He was afraid of feeling. Of
loss. More loss after years and years of it.

But his father had died without knowing. Without
knowing that even though things weren't always the
best between them, Sam had loved him. Elizabeth
had died without knowing Sam had cared.

Protecting himself meant hurting other people.
And it damn well hurt him.

Maddy had been brave enough to show him. And
he had rejected it. Utterly. Completely. She had been
so brave, and he had remained shut down as he'd
been for years.

She had removed any risk of rejection and still
he had been afraid. He had been willing to lose her
this time.

"Do you know why the art is hard?" he asked.

"Why?"

"Because. If I make what I really want to, then I
actually have to feel it."

He hated saying it. Hated admitting it. But he
knew, somehow, that this was essential to his soul.
That if he was ever going to move on from this place,
from this dry, drunken place that produced nothing

but anguish, he had to start saying these things. He had to start committing to these things.

"I had a lot behind this idea that I wasn't good enough. That I didn't deserve to feel. Because…the alternative is feeling it. It's caring when it's easier to be mad at everything. Hoping for things when so much is already dead."

"What's the alternative?" Chase asked.

He looked around his studio. At all the lifeless things. Hard and sharp. Just like he was. The alternative was living without hope. The alternative was acting like he was dead too.

"This," he said finally. "And life without Maddy. I'd rather risk everything than live without her."

Thirteen

Madison looked around the beautifully appointed room. The grand party facility at the ranch was decorated in evergreen boughs and white Christmas lights, the trays of glittering champagne moving by somehow adding to the motif. Sparkling. Pristine.

Maddy herself was dressed in a gown that could be described in much the same manner. A pale yellow that caught the lights and glimmered like sun on new-fallen snow.

However, it was a prime example of how appearances can be deceiving. She felt horrible. Much more like snow that had been mixed up with gravel. Gritty. Gray.

Hopefully no one was any the wiser. She was

good at putting on a brave face. Good at pretending everything was fine. Something she had perfected over the years. Not just at these kinds of public events but at family events too.

Self-protection was her favorite accessory. It went with everything.

She looked outside, at the terrace, which was lit by a thatch of Christmas lights, heated by a few free-standing heaters. However, no one was out there. She took a deep breath, seeing her opportunity for escape. And she took it. She just needed a few minutes. A few minutes to feel a little bit less like her face would crack beneath the weight of her fake smile.

A few minutes to take a deep breath and not worry so much that it would turn into a sob.

She grabbed hold of a glass of champagne, then moved quickly to the door, slipping out into the chilly night air. She went over near one of the heaters, wrapping her arms around herself and simply standing for a moment, looking out into the inky blackness, looking at nothing. It felt good. It was a relief to her burning eyes. A relief to her scorched soul.

All of this feelings business was rough. She wasn't entirely certain she could recommend it.

"What's going on, Maddy?"

She turned around, trying to force a smile when she saw her brother Gage standing there.

"I just needed a little bit of quiet," she said, lifting her glass of champagne.

"Sure." He stuffed his hands in his pockets. "I'm

not used to this kind of thing. I spent a lot of time on the road. In crappy hotels. Not a lot of time at these sorts of get-togethers."

"Regretting the whole return-of-the-prodigal-son thing? Because it's too late to unkill that fatted calf, young man. You're stuck."

He laughed. "No. I'm glad that I'm back. Because of you. Because of Colton, Sierra. Even Jack."

"Rebecca?"

"Of course." He took a deep breath, closing the distance between them. "So what's going on with you?"

"Nothing," she said, smiling.

"I have a feeling that everybody else usually buys that. Which is why you do it. But I don't. Is it Jack? Is it having him here?"

She thought about that. Seriously thought about it. "No," she said, truthful. "I'm glad. I'm so glad that we're starting to fix some of this. I spent a long time holding on to my anger. My anger at Dad. At the past. All of my pain. And Jack got caught up in that. Because of the circumstances. We are all very different people. And getting to this point...I feel like we took five different paths. But here we are. And it isn't for Dad. It's for us. I think that's good. I spent a lot of time doing things in response to him. In response to the pain that he caused me. I don't want to do that anymore. I don't want to act from a place of pain and fear anymore."

"That's quite a different stance. I mean, since last we talked at The Grind."

She tried to smile again, wandering over to one of the wooden pillars. "I guess some things happened." She pressed her palm against the cold surface, then her forehead. She took a deep breath. In and out, slowly, evenly.

"Are you okay?"

She shook her head. "Not really. But I will be."

"I know I missed your first big heartbreak. And I feel like I would have done that bastard some bodily harm. I have quite a bit of internalized rage built up. If you need me to hurt anyone…I will. Gladly."

She laughed. "I appreciate that. Really, I do. It's just that…it's a good thing this is happening. It's making me realize a lot of things. It's making me change a lot of things. I just wish it didn't hurt."

"You know…when Rebecca told me that she loved me, it scared the hell out of me. And I said some things that I shouldn't have said. That no one should ever say to anyone. I regretted it. But I was running scared, and I wanted to make sure she didn't come after me. I'm so glad that she forgave me when I realized what an idiot I was."

She lifted her head, turning to face him. "That sounds a lot like brotherly advice."

"It is. And maybe it's not relevant to your situation. I don't know. But what I do know is that we both have a tendency to hold on to pain. On to anger. If you get a chance to fix this, I hope you forgive the bastard. As long as he's worthy."

"How will I know he's worthy?" she asked, a bit of humor lacing her voice.

"Well, I'll have to vet him. At some point."

"Assuming he ever speaks to me again, I would be happy to arrange that."

Gage nodded. "If he's half as miserable as you are, trust me, he'll be coming after you pretty quick."

"And you think I should forgive him?"

"I think that men are a bunch of hardheaded dumb-asses. And some of us need more chances than others. And I thank God every day I got mine. With this family. With Rebecca. So it would be mean-spirited of me not to advocate for the same for another of my species."

"I'll keep that under advisement."

Gage turned to go. "Do that. But if he keeps being a dumbass, let me know. Because I'll get together a posse or something."

"Thank you," she said. "Hopefully the posse won't be necessary."

He shrugged, then walked back into the party. She felt fortified then. Because she knew she had people on her side. No matter what. She wasn't alone. And that felt good. Even when most everything felt bad.

She let out a long, slow breath and rested her forearms on the railing, leaning forward, staring out across the darkened field. If she closed her eyes, she could almost imagine that she could see straight out to the ocean in spite of the fact that it was dark.

She was starting to get cold, even with the artificial heat. But it was entirely possible the chill was coming from inside her. Side effects of heartbreak and all of that.

"Merry Christmas Eve."

She straightened, blinking, looking out into the darkness. Afraid to turn around. That voice was familiar. And it didn't belong to anyone in her family.

She turned slowly, her heart stalling when she saw Sam standing there. He was wearing a white shirt unbuttoned at the collar, a black jacket and a pair of black slacks. His hair was disheveled, and she was pretty sure she could see a bit of soot on his chest where the open shirt exposed his skin.

"What are you doing here?"

"I had to see you." He took a step closer to her. "Bad enough that I put this on."

"Where did you get it?"

"The secondhand store on Main."

"Wow." No matter what he had to say, the fact that Sam McCormack had shown up in a suit said a whole lot without him ever opening his mouth.

"It doesn't really fit. And I couldn't figure out how to tie the tie." And of course, he hadn't asked anyone for help. Sam never would. It just wasn't him.

"Well, then going without was definitely the right method."

"I have my moments of brilliance." He shook his head. "But the other day wasn't one of them."

Her heart felt as if it were in a free fall, her stomach clenching tight. "Really?"

"Yeah."

"I agree. I mean, unreservedly. But I am open to hearing about your version of why you didn't think you were brilliant. Just in case we have differing opinions on the event."

He cursed. "I'm not good at this." He took two steps toward her, then reached out, gripping her chin between his thumb and forefinger. "I hate this, in fact. I'm not good at talking about feelings. And I've spent a lot of years trying to bury them down deep. I would like to do it now. But I know there's no good ending to that. I know that I owe you more."

"Go on," she said, keeping her eyes on his, her voice trembling, betraying the depth of emotion she felt.

She had never seen Sam quite like this, on edge, like he might shatter completely at any moment. "I told you I thought I didn't deserve these feelings. And I believed it."

"I know you did," she said, the words broken. "I know that you never lied on purpose, Sam. I know."

"I don't deserve that. That certainty. I didn't do anything to earn it."

She shook her head. "Stop. We're not going to talk like that. About what we deserve. I don't know what I deserve. But I know what I want. I want you.

And I don't care if I'm jumping the gun. I don't care if I didn't make you grovel enough. It's true. I do."

"Maddy…"

"This all comes because we tried to protect ourselves for too long. Because we buried everything down deep. I don't have any defenses anymore. I can't do it anymore. I couldn't even if I wanted to. Which you can see, because I'm basically throwing myself at you again."

"I've always been afraid there was something wrong with me." His dark eyes were intense, and she could tell that he was wishing he could turn to stone rather than finish what he was saying. But that he was determined. That he had put his foot on the path and he wasn't going to deviate from it. "Something wrong with what I felt. And I pushed it all down. I always have. I've been through stuff that would make a lot of people crazy. But if you keep shoving it on down, it never gets any better." He shook his head. "I've been holding on to grief. Holding on to anger. I didn't know what else to do with it. My feelings about my parents, my feelings about Elizabeth, the baby. It's complicated. It's a lot. And I think more than anything I just didn't want to deal with it. I had a lot of excuses, and they felt real. They even felt maybe a little bit noble?"

"I can see that. I can see it being preferable to grief."

"Just like you said, Maddy. You put all those

defenses in front of it, and then nothing can hurt you, right?"

She nodded. "At least, that's been the way I've handled it for a long time."

"You run out. Of whatever it is you need to be a person. Whatever it is you need to contribute, to create. That's why I haven't been able to do anything new with my artwork." He rolled his eyes, shaking his head slightly. "It's hard for me to…"

"I know. You would rather die than talk about feelings. And talk about this. But I think you need to."

"I told myself it was wrong to make something for my dad. My mom. Because they didn't support my work. I told myself I didn't deserve to profit off Elizabeth's death in any way. But that was never the real issue. The real issue was not wanting to feel those things at all. I was walking across the field the other night, and I thought about grief. The way that it covers things, twists the world around you into something unrecognizable." He shook his head. "When you're in the thick of it, it's like walking in the dark. Even if you're in a place you've seen a thousand times by day, it all changes. And suddenly what seemed safe is now full of danger."

He took a sharp breath and continued. "You can't trust anymore. You can't trust everything will be okay, because you've seen that sometimes it isn't. That's what it's like to have lost people like I have. And I can think about a thousand pieces that I could create that would express that. But it would mean that I had to feel it. And it would mean I would have to show other people what I felt. I wanted… From the moment I laid my hands on you, Maddy, I wanted to turn you into something. A sculpture. A painting. But that would mean looking at how I felt about you too. And I didn't want to do that either."

Maddy lifted her hand, cupping Sam's cheek. "I understand why you work with iron, Sam. Because it's just like you. You're so strong. And you really don't want to bend. But if you would just bend…just a little bit, I think you could be something even more beautiful than you already are."

"I'll do more than bend. If I have to, to have you, I'll break first. But I've decided… I don't care about protecting myself. From loss, from pain…doesn't matter. I just care about you. And I know that I have to fix myself if I'm going to become the kind of man you deserve. I know I have to reach inside and figure all that emotional crap out. I can't just decide that I love you and never look at the rest of it. I have to do all of it. To love you the way that you deserve, I know I have to deal with all of it."

"Do you love me?"

He nodded slowly. "I do." He reached into his jacket pocket and took out a notebook. "I've been working on a new collection. Just sketches right now. Just plans." He handed her the notebook. "I want you to see it. I know you'll understand."

She took it from him, opening it with shaking

hands, her heart thundering hard in her throat. She looked at the first page, at the dark twisted mass he had sketched there. Maybe it was a beast, or maybe it was just menacing angles—it was hard to tell. She imagined that was the point.

There was more. Broken figures, twisted metal. Until the very last page. Where the lines smoothed out into rounded curves, until the mood shifted dramatically and everything looked a whole lot more like hope.

"It's hard to get a sense of scale and everything in the drawings. This is just me kind of blocking it out."

"I understand," she whispered. "I understand perfectly." It started with grief, and it ended with love. Unimaginable pain that was transformed.

"I lost a lot of things, Maddy. I would hate for you to be one of them. Especially because you're the one thing I chose to lose. And I have regretted it every moment since. But this is me." He put his fingertip on the notebook. "That's me. I'm not the nicest guy. I'm not what anybody would call cheerful. Frankly, I'm a grumpy son of a bitch. It's hard for me to talk about what I'm feeling. Harder for me to show it, and I'm in the world's worst line of work for that. But if you'll let me, I'll be your grumpy son of a bitch. And I'll try. I'll try for you."

"Sam," she said, "I love you. I love you, and I don't need you to be anything more than you. I'm willing to accept the fact that getting to your feelings may always be a little bit of an excavation. But if you promise to work on it, I'll promise not to be

too sensitive about it. And maybe we can meet somewhere in the middle. One person doesn't have to do
all the changing. And I don't want you to anyway."
She smiled, and this time it wasn't forced. "You had
me at 'You're at the wrong door.'"

He chuckled. "I think you had me a lot sooner
than that. I just didn't know it."

"So," she said, looking up at him, feeling like the
sun was shining inside her, in spite of the chill outside, "you want to go play Yahtzee?"

"Only if you mean it euphemistically."

"Absolutely not. I expect you to take the time
to woo me, Sam McCormack. And if that includes
board games, that's just a burden you'll have to bear."

Sam smiled. A real smile. One that showed his
heart, his soul, and held nothing back. "I would
gladly spend the rest of my life bearing your bur-
dens, Madison West."

"On second thought," she said, "board games not
required."

"Oh yeah? What do you need, then?"

"Nothing much at all. Just hold me, cowboy.
That's enough for me."

* * * * *

Meet all the cowboys in Copper Ridge!

Look for more **COPPER RIDGE** *books,
coming soon!*

*If you can't get enough Maisey Yates,
try her bestselling books
from Harlequin Presents!*

Don't miss
THE PRINCE'S PREGNANT MISTRESS
Second in her fabulous
HEIRS BEFORE VOWS *series.*
Available next month!

*If you're on Twitter, tell us what you think of
Harlequin Desire! #harlequindesire*